DEVO MANNIX

THE SORCERER'S APPRENTICE

BOOKS BY ROLAND BOIKE

THE MAN WHO REMEMBERED TOO MUCH
***
THE MAN WHO COULD NOT REMEMBER
***
THE CAVE OF FORGOTTEN DREAMS
***
PORTAL TO ANOTHER UNIVERSE
***
YOU ARE NOT AMANDA MARTIN

WHAT DO YOU REALLY WANT?
***
FINDING AUNT BETH
***
THE RING OF DEATH
***
OPPORTUNITIES
***
THE WAGER

CHILDREN'S BOOKS
THE DEVO MANNIX SERIES

CASTING SPELLS - BOOK 1

CARS AND CATS - BOOK 2

WHAT ARE FRIENDS FOR - BOOK 3

DANGEROUS ADVENTURES - BOOK 4

SPIRITS FROM THE PAST - BOOK 5

THE DISAPPEARING CAT - BOOK 6

DOGNAPERS BOOK - 7

WISHES - BOOK 8

DEVO MANNIX

THE SORCERER'S APPRENTICE

CASTING SPELLS

ROLAND V. BOIKE

Martin and Bowman
1-855-921-1348

This Book is dedicated
to my daughter Carolyn A Kenney
A constant inspiration for me.

Contents

Chapter 1

A SPELL TO MAKE IT RAIN

It had not rained in the White Rock Mountains in Brown County for over two months; flowers were wilting, farmers were losing their crops and all the trees were dropping their leaves.

It was normally dry at this time of the year but this dry spell had continued without rain longer than any other dry spell in Brown County's recorded history. To complicate the matter, the temperature had risen to new record highs.

Early one August morning, Devo and his grandfather, Sargo Mannix, were sitting on the front porch of their family farmhouse watching the morning sunrise over the White Rock Mountains. Devo and Sargo were discussing the present drought.

Devo's thoughts suddenly turned to his Grandfather. "You are by far the most notable and respected sorcerer in all of the Americas and possibly of the world. Is there something you might be able to do; perhaps some magical summons you might perform that would cause it to rain?" Devo asked his grandfather.

"I am sure there is something I can do, perform, say, or someone I can call upon; some being from another world that will cause it to rain; however, you must be aware that all magical acts set in motion a chain reaction that not only does good but may also cause some bad," Grandfather said.

"I do not understand Grandfather, if you make it rain how could that be bad?" Devo asked.

"Well, tell me, Devo what good do you think might come from the rain that I cause to fall upon Brown County?"

"It would save the flowers and the trees, it would save the farmers crops, it would wash the dust from the streets and the stores could sell more raincoats and umbrellas," Devo said.

"Think about this Devo, Grandfather said, what about the Johnson's family picnic, it may be too wet for them to go to the park; what about Harold Wilson who spent all morning washing his car and don't forget Steve Kramer the farmer who just cut his *alfalfa* this morning and has it drying in the sun. How about the owner of the Bishop Building downtown, they just finished washing two stories of windows, how do you think they will feel about my rain?"

"I did not think about that," Devo said.

"And remember this; once you set off your magical spell or give a command to change the things about you, it will remain forever and no other person's magic can undo the spell, not even you. That is why a lot of thought must go into casting a spell before you start changing the world around you."

"I did not know that, Grandfather," Devo said.

The two sat on the porch for a long time; finally, Grandfather got up and said, "Devo I am going into the house and do some studying in my *Book of Magic and Incantations* to help me decide if I should take a hand in this drought and make it rain."

The Book of Magic and Incantations.

"See you later Grandfather. I am going to play with Speeler," Devo said.

Grandfather went into the house and Devo went into the back yard to greet his dog, Speeler.

"Hi! Speeler, want to play ball?" Devo asked.

Speeler jumped up and leaned against Devo's chest with his two front paws.

As Devo leaned over to pet his dog, Speeler became so excited to see his friend that he barked several times and licked Devo's hand.

Picking up a stick, Devo waved it above his head a number of times and then threw it as hard as he could into the back yard.

Speeler barked and leaped into action chasing the stick as it flew through the air to the edge of the woods. Speeler almost caught the stick before it hit the ground. He grabbed the stick in his mouth, held it firmly in his teeth and ran back to Devo. Speeler laid the stick at Devo's feet and barked. Speeler was excited and was waiting for Devo to pick up the stick which was now wet with Speeler's saliva.

Panting and with his tongue hanging out, Speeler made ready for Devo to throw the stick again.

The two played until it grew very hot and by that time, they both were sweating and thirsty.

Devo took Speeler back to the house and filled his doggie dish with fresh water; then Devo got himself a cool drink from the garden hose.

Devo and his dog went to the front porch and after lunch, Devo played with his soldiers while Speeler slept.

At dinner, Devo asked his grandfather if he had made a decision on making it rain.

"I am still reading my book on magic and incantations," Grandfather said.

"Do you think you will make a decision soon Grandfather?" Devo asked.

"Probably some time tonight, long after you have gone to sleep Devo. I need to give this some serious thought," Grandfather said.

"I will need to make just the correct amount of rain that will do the least amount of harm and give the greatest benefits."

"I will need to check my calculations several times again before I make a final decision," Grandfather said.

After dinner, Devo went to his room, did his homework, showered and read a few pages of the Box Car Kids. When he had finished his nightly routine Devo went down to the kitchen, kissed his mother and father goodnight and headed off to bed.

"If you see Grandfather tell him I said goodnight and I hope he will make it rain tonight," Devo said.

Devo climbed the spiral stairs to his room, turned off the light and crawled into bed.

Devo reached under his spare pillow and pulled out his flashlight and his book. He read about the Box Car Children in the darkness of his room using his flashlight. Devo knew if his parents passed his room and saw light coming out from under the door, they would check his room to see if there was a problem.

Even though it was his regular bedtime, Devo did not feel sleepy. He decided instead to stay up and read. Devo was hoping that he would be awake so that he could hear the rain falling on the roof above his bedroom; if his grandfather decided to make it rain.

Devo lay there in bed thinking about all the people in Brown County and elsewhere who were suffering from the drought.

I know that Grandfather will make it rain this evening. I think that probably is the only course of action left for him. Just imagine how much good it will do, Devo thought.

When Devo grew tired, he turned off the flashlight, put his page marker in his book, slipped the book and the flashlight back under the spare pillow and went to sleep.

A thundering boom awakened Devo from a deep sleep and caused him to sit up in bed in the dark of the night. At first, he thought an airplane had come crashing into the house or perhaps one of the trees by his bedroom window had fallen on the roof.

Suddenly the whole room was lit up and Devo could see everything in the room including his books and his toys lying in one corner of his bedroom. Before he could catch his breath there was another loud boom, this time almost as loud as if he had been standing at the end of the muzzle of a cannon that had just fired a shell into the air.

It was only after the third flash of lightning and the loud exploding burst of thunder that followed that Devo realized there was a severe thunderstorm occurring just outside his bedroom window.

The wind was blowing so hard he could hear the shutters bang against the house and the garden gate crash against the tool shed. It sounded at times as though some of the shingles might come off the roof. The wind and rain were now pounding against Devo's window. The rain was so heavy it seemed as though someone was holding a hose against the panes of glass and running water in a steady stream.

Three more bright flashes of lightning; three loud rumbling clashes of thunder and Devo was out of his bed standing on the floor in his bare feet.

It was then that Devo thought of Speeler and wondered if his dog was alright.

I wonder if Speeler is as frightened as I am Devo thought?

Devo walked across the room in his pajamas and bare feet and down the hall to the stairs. As he walked down the spiral staircase, the flashes of lightning cast an eerie shadow of Devo on the wall.

Devo went to the front door, unfastened the lock and opened the door. There on the front porch sitting as close to the door as he could possibly get; sat Speeler wagging his tail and panting with his tongue hanging out of his mouth.

Without invitation, Speeler ran into the house, up the stairs and headed for Devo's bed.

Devo closed the door, fastened the lock, turned and ran up the stairs with all the speed he could muster. Devo jumped in bed and snuggled up to Speeler, who already seemed to be asleep under the covers.

The storm continued for some time but the lightning and thunder went unnoticed by Devo, as he lay nuzzled up against Speeler. Devo put his arm around Speeler and said, "I feel safe when I am with you Speeler, do you feel safer when you are with me?" Devo whispered to his dog so as not to awaken his parents or grandfather.

Speeler gave Devo's hand a couple of licks with his moist tongue and went back to sleep.

"I take that to be a "Yes" Speeler," Devo said.

Chapter 2

THE BOOK OF MAGIC AND INCANTATIONS

Devo lay there in bed snuggled up close to his Speeler, Devo thought how much fun he could have if Speeler could talk to him and understand what he said. I could tell Speeler to go and get things for me and he would understand what I said, "That would be…N… E…A… T!

"Just think if some big kid at school threatens me, I could tell Speeler exactly what to do."

Devo lay there in bed and continued to think of the many possibilities and advantages if he could talk to his dog and his dog could talk to him.

The storm seemed to pass and only a slight rumble of thunder could be heard in the distance as Devo lay on the bed with his best friend, Speeler.

"Just think of it Speeler, you and I could have so much fun if only you could talk and understand me. We could play hide and go seek, you could tell me about your life as a dog; what you see, smell and how things taste. I might even teach you to play a board game like Checkers or Monopoly, wouldn't that be fun?" Devo told Speeler.

"I have it, Devo said out loud. Come with me Speeler, I have a great idea."

Devo jumped from the bed and Speeler followed him down the stairs in the dark to his grandfather's library. Devo entered the room and turned on the desk lamp. He pulled up a chair for Speeler to sit in.

"I want you to sit in this chair Speeler, be quiet, no barking or whining. You just sit and watch what I am about to do."

"If Grandfather can make it rain, I can make you talk and understand me Speeler," Devo said as he patted his dog on the head.

Devo knew that his grandfather used the big leather book that sat in the middle of his desk to perform his spells and magical incantations. He had seen him open the book on numerous occasions and work the magic that was written in the pages of the big leather-bound volume.

As Devo opened the book, he noticed a large red leather bookmark with a red silk tassel inserted into one of the pages. He held the bookmark in place and opened the book to see what his grandfather read that was so important that it caused him to mark the page.

At the top of the page written in Old English calligraphy, Devo saw a large "**R**" Each subject was marked by underlined black letters with titles like Rainbow, Reindeer, Rage, Rats and Remember.

At the very top of the page, the very first magical spell was **RAIN.** There followed after a list of spells that could be cast concerning rain. There was a small piece of notepaper, which had writing on it.

Two-and one-half inches of rain dropped in one-and one-half hours, winds up to 60 miles per hours, more than normal amount of electrical activity.

Devo turned the pages until he found "**S**." He ran his finger down the page until he found **SPEECH.** Devo sat and read all the incantations that could be cast concerning speech. About half way down the printed subject matter, he read how to give speech to objects. Devo pulled himself close to the desk and leaned over as far as he could to read what was printed in the book.

"Ah! There it is Speeler," Devo said.

Devo leaned over and pulled the desk lamp close so he could read the words printed in the *Book of Magic and Incantations.*

After Devo read all the instructions, he turned to Speeler and said, "Are you ready Speeler? I shall read it aloud for you and then do what it says."

"How to make animals speak and understand.

You must assemble the following:

Three candles, triangular shaped white cloth, a white circle of cloth that will fit within the triangle and an item belonging to the subject. Place the triangular shaped white cloth on the table. Place a lighted candle on each point of the triangle.

Cut a round circle from the material used for making the triangle. Inscribe the words Speech and Comprehend on the round circle seven times."

Devo went out to the dining room and removed three candles from the buffet along with a pack of safety matches. Devo took the candles back to his grandfather's den and placed them on the desk.

Devo took two pieces of white paper from the computer's printer. He cut one triangle and one circle from the paper. He placed the triangle on his grandfather's desk, put a candle on each point and lit them.

Devo wrote the words Speech and Comprehend on the round circle seven times.

Following the directions, Devo placed the circle on Speeler's mouth briefly, then momentarily on Speeler's head and ears, then he placed it in the center of the triangle.

Devo removed some hair from Speeler's back and placed it in the center of the circle. Devo was now ready to cast the spell.

Devo read on. There are five things that the Conjurer must do to cast the spell of speech on animals.

1. The animal's head should be at eye level of the Conjurer. Look the beast in the eye while you are performing the incantation.
2. The Conjurer shall place the round circle with the words Speech and Comprehend, briefly on the head and the ears of the beast and then place it in the center of the triangle. Place the item belonging to the subject in the center of the circle.

3. The Conjurer shall cup both hands over the mouth of the animal while calling upon Erebos, the God of darkness, asking to have speech given to the animal so it may talk.

4. The Conjurer shall cup both hands over the ears of the animal while calling upon Tartarus, the God of shadows, asking to give hearing to the animal so it may understand the spoken word.

5. The Conjurer must tap the head of the animal seven times while saying Erebos and Tartarus, I command you to fulfill my wishes.

*Caution: This spell cannot be undone. The animal will understand the spoken word and will have the ability to talk forever in its lifetime.

Devo was now ready to perform the five tasks that the spell required. He went over to Speeler and while looking him in the eye, he placed his hands on Speeler's mouth, then on his head and said, "Oh! Erebos and Tartarus, I command you to fulfill my wishes, Oh! Erebos and Tartarus, I command you to fulfill my wishes." Devo said the magic words the required seven times as set forth in Grandfather's book of magic.

For one brief moment, Speeler was surrounded with a halo of green shimmering light. Speeler gave an involuntary quiver and then looking at Devo he barked, "Man that was eerie. I'm hungry, think I'll go to the kitchen and get something to eat. Any chance I can get a wiener or some lunchmeat from the refrigerator, Devo? I hate that dry dog food you have been feeding me,"

Devo was so stunned he just stood there in silence and shook his head. He finally regained his faculties and said "I don't' think so Speeler."

Speeler made a beeline for the kitchen and was gone from sight before Devo could utter another word. Devo closed up Grandfather's book of magic, threw the triangle and circle in the waste container, replaced the candles, turned off the lights and went upstairs to bed.

It was quite a while before Speeler jumped up on the bed and snuggled up next to Devo.

"Stay on your side of the bed and don't hog the covers tonight. I get cold with the air conditioning on when I sleep in the house at night," Speeler barked.

"I always try not to crowd you in bed at night, Speeler and I shall try to see that you have covers to keep you warm."

"Well, see that you do; there is going to be some changes around here if I have my way. I am tired and I am going to sleep so don't stay up all night and try to talk to me," Speeler barked in a clear authoritative voice.

Devo was stunned by his dog's attitude, but since Speeler was his best friend, he thought he would give him some lead way and they both soon fell asleep.

In the morning, Devo awoke when the sun was just breaking over the top of the White Rock Mountains. He looked on the bed and around the room but Speeler was nowhere to be found.

Devo got out of bed, dressed, washed his face and went downstairs to find Speeler, as he was anxious to talk to his friend. He had so many questions to ask him and it would be great to get some perspective on how dogs saw the world. Speeler was nowhere to be found. Devo asked his mother, father and his grandfather if they had seen Speeler.

Devo's mother said, "I let Speeler out this morning when I got up to make coffee for your dad and grandfather. I haven't seen him since."

Devo ate breakfast hurriedly and ran out the door into the yard to find Speeler.

"Here Speeler, here Speeler, here Speeler," Devo called, but Speeler did not answer the call.

Devo looked in all of Speeler's favorite places, the dog house, under the front porch, under the Lilac bush on the side of the house and on the floor in the barn; Speeler was nowhere to be found.

Devo felt very bad about the disappearance of his best friend and he wondered if he had made a mistake giving his dog the ability to talk and understand the language.

Devo sat on the front porch for a long time. Grandfather finally came out the front porch screen door and sat down next to Devo on the steps.

"You seem unhappy today Devo, is there something bothering you?" Grandfather asked.

"Speeler has been gone all morning and I am afraid that he might be in trouble and need me."

"I would not worry Devo, sometimes dogs just need to get away, be on their own and explore their world. He probably is somewhere in the neighborhood sniffing every tree and bush and smelling all the trash cans that have been placed at the curb for pickup today."

Devo thought maybe he should tell his grandfather he had made his dog talk and Speeler's attitude toward him seemed to have changed, but at the last minute, he changed his mind as he thought this was not the right time or place to let Grandfather know he had used his book of magic without permission.

Devo went into the house and brought some of his toy soldiers and hot wheels out to the porch steps to play with while he waited for Speeler to return.

Devo's parents were going to do the weekly grocery shopping and run a few errands after lunch.

Devo loved to shop with his mother because if he was especially good, she always rewarded him with a small toy or an ice cream cone on a hot day.

"I want to stay here and wait for Speeler today. I want to be home when he gets here, Mom," Devo said.

"I want to make sure he is okay when he comes back."

Chapter 3

A BAD DAY AT WHITE ROCK

It was almost noon when Devo saw the butcher, Mr. Hanna of Hanna's Butcher Shop pull into the drive. He got out of his car and walked up to Devo who was sitting on the porch steps.

"Is your father home Devo?" he asked.

"No Mr. Hanna, he is at work and will not be home until after five."

"Ask your father if he will call me at the butcher shop when he gets home; I need to talk to him about your dog."

"Our dog?... Is there something wrong with our dog?"

"Your dog came into the butcher shop this morning when Mr. Cummings was just leaving the shop after picking up his meat order. I looked over the meat counter and saw a dog enter my shop I did not immediately recognize, I said, "Get out of here you mangy mutt. Dogs are not allowed in butcher shops."

"I thought the dog said something to me and since I know dogs do not talk, it really scared me. In a state of shock and disbelief, I instinctively threw my meat-tenderizing hammer at him and told him to get out."

"Then that dog ran behind the meat counter, grabbed my pant leg and pulled so hard on it he tore my pants."

"It was then that I recognized the dog and knew he belonged to your family. He is the one you always come into the butcher shop with. I'd say your dog has Rabies and should be put away."

Devo looked at Mr. Hanna in disbelief wondering what had become of his dog. Devo could not remember Speeler ever growling at anyone, let alone attacking them.

"I am so sorry Mr. Hanna, are you sure it was Speeler?"

"Yes, I am sure, small, brown and white male dog, two black hind paws, one black and one white front paw."

"That does sound like Speeler," Devo said as he took a deep breath.

"Well, that's not the worst of it. Arnie, the mailman was just coming in the butcher shop door with the morning mail when I threw the meat-tenderizing hammer at your dog. Your dog was yelping and Arnie Kinkel thought that a mad dog was about to attack him. Arnie grabbed his can of mace and sprayed the dog as he ran past him."

"In the excitement, Arnie dropped his mailbag. The mail fell out of his bag and the wind blew most of it into a water puddle at the edge of the curb."

"Then that crazed dog ran into the street and when Mr. Willacher saw him, he slammed on his brakes and skidded into the fire hydrant," Mr. Hanna said.

"Water squirted up all over the place from the broken fire hydrant and the mail that was in the roadway washed into the drain at the side of the road," Mr. Hanna said.

"Well, tell your father I was here and have him call me," Mr. Hanna said as he turned and walked back to his car in the drive.

Oh, what have I done, Devo thought, this is not going well. I just wanted a pal that could talk to me; what have I done?

Devo jumped up and decided it was time to take action and go into town, find Speeler and keep him out of trouble.

Devo opened the front door and called to his mother, "Mom I am going to walk down the block to see if I can find Speeler; I won't be long."

"OK honey," his mother called back, "Don't stay too long; lunch will be in about one hour."

Devo had walked about two blocks calling his dog, "Here Speeler, here Speeler, here Speeler."

Suddenly from under one of the bushes at the edge of the park Speeler appeared.

"Speeler, where on earth have you been? I have been looking everywhere for you; I was worried about you."

"I don't appreciate you calling me by saying "Here Speeler!" and besides it's none of your business where I have been," Speeler barked in a very angry tone.

"Speeler, why are you so angry and why are you talking to me so mean?" Devo asked.

"Well buddy, you are the one that caused me to talk and now that I understand the meaning of things people are saying to me why wouldn't I be mean?"

"Mean to you, who is mean to you?" Devo asked.

"Well to start with I was relieving myself in the neighbor's yard when that grumpy old man that lives with his wife in that dilapidated old house on Taylor Street threw his newspaper at me and called me some names, I am too polite to mention. When he threw his morning newspaper at me, which I might mention hit me in the head, he was yelling get out of here you ugly mutt."

"Later, I went into the grocery store to take a look around to see if I could find anything to eat; that is when some smart aleck kid took me to the back of the store, opened the back door and kicked me off the dock.

I fell into a pile of decomposing cabbage leaves from the produce department and got green slime all over me. I smelled like a skunk so, I went over to the fountain at City Hall and jumped into the water to wash the green slime off of me. I was just getting out of the pool and shaking off when that police officer; you know the one that told you I had to be on a leash; came up and for no reason at all hit me in the rear end with his nightstick. I yelped and ran off.

So, I was running down Main Street as fast as I could trying to avoid any humans that might be out that early in the morning, when I suddenly found myself in front of Hanna's Butcher Shop."

"Well, you always go in there and talk to that nice man, so why not me? Just about the time I got to the door, that Cummings man came out and I walked in while the door was open.

I walked up to the meat case and asked Mr. Hanna if he had a spare bone he could give to me to save me from an untimely death from starvation.

You would have thought a bomb went off in his face. His mouth flew open, his eyelids opened up so wide I thought his eyeballs were going to drop out. He made a yelping sound and threw his arms up into the air. In his right hand, he had some kind of metal hammer that he threw at me. It was just my misfortune, just as it had been all morning; the object he threw at me struck me in the head."

"You know by this time I was getting annoyed at humans mistreating me so I decided I would put a stop to it and let people know I was not to be trifled with. I scooted behind the meat counter and grabbed Mr. Hanna by the pants cuff, bit down with my teeth as hard as I could, shook my head and growled like a dog.

In my defense, I must say that I was still dazed from the blow on the head and did not quite realize what I was doing.

Mr. Hanna reached over and grabbed me by the collar as I hung onto his pants cuff. While hunched over, Mr. Hanna ran over to the open door of the butcher shop and kicked as hard as he possibly could in an attempt to remove me from his leg. I lost my grip on his pant leg and went flying through the air. He had some unkind words that he said to me as I hit the pavement in the street."

"As I was flying through the air, I passed the mailman, who had been standing in the doorway and witnessed the whole episode. He had removed his spray can of mace from his mail pouch and can you believe; he sprayed my eyes with the mace as I flew past him. I could not see anything; my eyesight was blurred but I knew I had to get out of there."

"I headed for the alley across the street, running as fast as I could; thinking I could hide there until I could see where I was going. I still could not see but when I was about halfway across the street, I heard the squealing of tires and a crash. I knew someone had an automobile accident. I knew there was a lot going on so when I reached the alley, I stayed hidden behind some cardboard boxes."

"I heard police, fire sirens and a lot of voices coming from across the street. With my eyes still blurred I couldn't see a thing.

I knew better than to attempt to go back across the street so I went through the other end of the alley, behind some buildings."

"Thinking I would be safe now, I started heading for home," Speeler barked. "My eyes were still burning and I could hardly see. I knew the direction I needed to go to get home.

"I felt something wet and sandy between my toes. and that's when I felt the big end of a shovel hit me in the butt.

I Felt Something Wet And Sandy Between My Toes

The blow lifted me off of the ground; I yelped a few times and ran as hard as I could.

"Curse you dog! You ran through my new cement sidewalk, now I may have to redo the whole thing to get your footprints out of it," one of the workers said.

"I still could not see very well and I did not know who was yelling at me but I kept running as fast as I could, hoping I wouldn't run into a brick wall or a tree," Speeler barked.

"I finally ended up here in the park and I got under this bush planning to stay there until I could see where I was going. It was shortly after that I ran into you," Speeler barked.

"It is hard for me to believe that you have gotten into so much trouble so soon, Speeler. Are you sure that you did not bring your misfortune upon yourself?" Devo asked.

"No! Nope, No, I didn't do anything, Nope, No, I am sure, not me, No, I didn't do anything, and I am innocent. Speeler grumbled as he shook his head to signify a No."

"Let's go home, we will need to tell Dad what has happened to you today," Devo said.

"You are going to squeal on me, you are going to rat me out, some friend you turned out to be," Speeler barked.

Devo said nothing, as he reached over, put Speeler's leash on his collar and started to walk his dog home. It was very quiet as Devo and Speeler walked down the sidewalk toward home, neither one spoke out loud. Devo was pondering over his use of Grandfather's *Book of Magic and Incantations* and the unfortunate consequences that have followed.

Speeler on the other hand was wondering why people were so mean to him and abused him; after all, he had done nothing to deserve such treatment.

Speeler kept mumbling. "No! Nope, No, I didn't do anything, Nope, No, I am sure, not me, No, I didn't do anything, and I am innocent."

As Speeler looked down the sidewalk, he saw that grumpy old man that lives with his wife in that dilapidated old house on Taylor Street. He was the same old man hat had thrown his newspaper at him earlier in the day.

The old man and his wife were walking arm and arm down the sidewalk toward them. Devo and Speeler had to walk in the grass to pass them and as they did Speeler barked, "Hey you! Grumpy Old Man, why don't you and that Old Lady of yours move over so someone else can walk on the sidewalk other than you?"

Mrs. Thompson knowing that dogs do not talk, stopped; while still holding her husband's hand and said, "Devo that was very rude to say to my husband and me. I shall tell your mother the next time that I see her at bridge club and you had better keep that dog on a lease and out of our yard or I shall call the dog shelter and have him taken away. He is a horrible little dog!"

Mrs. Thompson gave her husband a tug on his arm and the two of them continued down the sidewalk. Devo could still hear Mrs. Thompson mumbling to her husband about Devo and his dog until her voice finally faded out in the distance.

Chapter 4

ORDERING ICE CREAM

Devo had been so shocked by Speeler's comment that he found himself speechless. The first thing that popped into his head was what have I done? I have made my dog and best friend into something rude and offensive and I am getting the blame for his actions.

Just about that time Speeler raised his ears as he picked up the sound of the ice cream truck just turning the corner on Elm Street heading their way.

"Boy oh boy, oh boy, Speeler barked. Here comes the ice cream truck," Speeler ran to the center of the street pulling Devo behind him in an effort to stop the ice cream man.

Here Comes The Ice Cream Truck

When the truck stopped, the driver opened his side panel and said, "How did you ever train your dog to do that trick?"

Before Devo could answer, Speeler ran up beneath the side panel of the truck and said, "Two Chocolate Drumsticks, please."

The attendant turned and before Devo could utter a word, the man had two Chocolate Drumsticks in his hand and was handing them to Devo.

"That will be three dollars and sixty cents."

"I do not want two drumsticks," Devo said emphatically.

"What do you want?"

"Make that two Eskimo pies," Speeler barked as he sat beneath the driver's window wagging his tail. The driver turned around placed the two drumsticks back in the freezer, grabbed two Eskimo pies and handed them out the window to Devo.

"That will be three dollars," the driver said.

"I don't want those Eskimo pies either," Devo said.

"Make up your mind Bud! What do you want?" The driver said in a disgruntled voice.

Once again from under the window Speeler called out, "I have made up my mind, I want the two Chocolate Drumsticks."

The driver replaced the two Eskimo pies in the freezer and took out two of the Chocolate Drumsticks.

"Like I said before, that will be three dollars and sixty cents."

It was too late to tell the attendant that he did not want the Drumsticks and that it was actually his dog who ordered them. Who would believe a story like that? Devo thought.

Reluctantly, Devo reached into his pocket and handed the man a five-dollar bill.

Devo put the change in his pocket, unwrapped one of the Drumsticks and laid it on the sidewalk for his friend Speeler to eat.

"Speeler, that was part of the money I was saving for my Mother's Day gift for my mom. That was very unkind of you to order something and make me pay for it."

"You know I don't have any money and if I did, how would I carry it, I don't have any pockets. Don't be so cheap kid, look at all the things I do for you."

Devo looked down at Speeler and said, "Speeler I think it best that you should keep your words and thoughts to yourself and do not speak unless you are spoken to."

"I think you need a change in attitude; you are getting me into a lot of trouble. I am not mad at you but I am very disappointed in your behavior this morning. I shall try to make allowances for you because it is your first day of speaking and understanding our language," Devo said.

"Hey, don't blame me Bud, you are responsible for making it so I can talk and understand what is said. It's not my fault; I am totally innocent. Why is everyone always picking on me? And you; you are supposed to be my best friend, why are you picking on me? Don't try to tell me what to do, what to say and when to say it." Speeler barked in a very annoyed tone.

"For the first time in my life I can understand what people are saying to me and about me. Sometimes I do not like what they say. This morning in the park, I was looking for someone who might throw a ball and I could chase it like I do with you. Well I saw this man and woman sitting on a blanket in the grass and he had a tennis ball, I went up to him, he put out his hand and I licked it only because he had the icing from a doughnut on his fingers. Then he started to scratch my head behind my ears, boy was I ever in pig heaven. Do you know what he said to me?"

"I am sure that I do not know Speeler but I'm also sure you will tell me," Devo said in sort of a disgusted voice.

"He said, "Well, you mangy mutt, I hope I don't get fleas or lice from you," then he took a "Wet One" and wiped his hands."

The woman sitting with him said, "Charlie you know better than to pet a stray dog, what if he bits you and he has Rabies."

"Yeah I know! Get out of here you ugly mutt," he said to me. Then he threw his shoe at me; I did not deserve that."

"I was about to turn around and bite him and his friend when I heard the ice cream truck going to the warehouse to load up all the ice-cream for this mornings' run. I ran as fast as I could to catch the ice cream man but, I did not catch him. I stopped at the butcher shop shortly after that."

"Well! You certainly had a busy morning Speeler. How will I explain all this to Mom and Dad? What will I tell Grandfather about you being able to talk?"

Devo and Speeler finally arrived home and Devo took Speeler to the back yard and chained him to the dog house.

"Hey, what do you think you are doing; don't chain me up here; I have a right to tell my side of the story," Speeler barked.

"Sorry Speeler but the only right you have at this point of your life are the rules that the S.P.C.A. enforce and I don't think they include an attorney for you or a jury that you can address so you may speak in your own defense."

"You are so unfair and I thought I was your friend. Remember all the sticks and balls I chased for you and remember all those thunderstorms when I kept you company so you would not be afraid; remember

all....t...h...e......t...i...m...e...s s...... s...... s."

Devo continued to walk towards the house and Speeler's voice slowly faded away until Devo reached the porch where he could only hear the occasional sound of the birds singing in the trees.

Devo sat on the porch for a long time with his head in his hands. "What am I to do? What am I to do?" He asked himself over and over.

Chapter 5

CONFIDING IN GRANDFATHER

Grandfather came out the front door of the house and sat down on the steps next to Devo.

"I thought you and Speeler would be at the baseball field this morning playing ball with your friends. You have been sitting on the porch for almost an hour with your head in your arms. Is there something the matter? Were you thrown out of the game? Have a fight with one of the boys? Are you not feeling well, Devo?"

Devo sat for a while without saying a word; he was not quite sure how to tell Grandfather or just where to start his tale of woe.

"W...e...l...l?" Grandfather asked in a tone that indicated to Devo that he was waiting on an answer.

"I do not know where to begin Grandfather; so much has happened to me since we sat here on the porch steps yesterday, I do not know what to tell you first."

"Well, just start at the beginning and tell me the important things that have caused you to be downhearted."

"Do you remember, you and I were sitting here on the steps and we talked about how dry it was and how badly we needed rain and I asked you if there was some magical thing that you could do to help the farmers and all the trees and plants that were affected by the drought?"

"Yes, I remember that very well Devo."

"Do you remember at dinner telling me that you were going to do some serious thinking on the problem after I was in bed sleeping?"

"Yes, I remember that very well Devo."

"Do you remember the storm we had that evening?" Well, I am sure you did! There was a real downpour and a lot of lightning and thunder that shook the house," Devo said.

I was so frightened, I went down and got Speeler who was sitting at the front door; I am sure he was frightened also. I let Speeler in and we both went up to my room and hid under the covers."

"I was so scared Grandfather; I was shaking and my heart was pounding. I thought I would be sick. I hugged Speeler and I told him how scared I was. Speeler just laid there and licked my hand for comfort. Then I thought how wonderful it would be if Speeler could talk to me and we could share our thoughts. I knew I would feel much better, I would not be so scared and I would have a friend and playmate that could talk and understand me."

"I am not quite sure what you have to worry about Devo, you have done nothing wrong. I am sure your mother and father would not object to Speeler being in bed with you one time during a very severe thunder storm when you were frightened."

"No, Grandfather, that is just where my troubles began."

There was a long pause in Devo's story of the events of the evening. Devo was trying to get his thoughts together to tell his grandfather about using his *Book of Magic and Incantations* without upsetting him.

Grandfather, I am hoping that you will forgive me for what I am about to tell you. I know now that I was wrong and I am so sorry for what I did."

There was another long pause in Devo's story; finally, Devo moved over very close to his grandfather and put his arms around him.

Tears started to swell in Devo's eyes and his throat grew very dry as he tenderly hugged his grandfather.

Grandfather put his arms around Devo as he spoke and gave him a soft warm hug. "Now, now, Devo! I know there is nothing that you have done which I will not forgive."

"Thank you, Grandfather, you know that I love you very much and I always try to do the things you teach me. I do not know if it was because I was so frightened or because I was so thrilled with the idea of Speeler talking and understanding me that I crept down to your library and opened your *Book of Magic and Incantations.*

"When I saw you had the book marker on the page entitled "RAIN" somehow I felt better about what I was doing. I thought you had used your powers to help the plants, animals, farmers and all the other people in Brown County. This made me feel better about looking up "SPEECH" and making Speeler talk and understand our language."

"As I look back on the events of the evening, I think I knew I had made a mistake because Speeler seemed to have changed. He was now telling me what to do, making his own decisions and now he talks continually."

"When Speeler realized he could talk and I could understand him he told me that he was going to the kitchen to eat, so I went to bed as I was very tired. Later that evening Speeler came into the bedroom and woke me up to tell me to, "Stay on your side of the bed and don't hog the covers tonight.

"I get cold when I sleep in the house at night when the air conditioner is on," Speeler barked at me.

"I told him I would be very careful about the blankets and then he told me to see that I did. Speeler told me there was going to be some changes around this household if he has his way. Then Grandfather, Speeler Barked he was tired and was going to sleep so I should not stay up all night and try to talk to him."

"When I woke up in the morning, Speeler was gone. I was not alarmed as I thought perhaps, he had gone to Lowbrook's Pond to chase Squirrel. Later in the day I went down the block to see if I could find Speeler. I was calling him when he suddenly came from under one of the bushes at the edge of the park. When Speeler appeared, I was so happy to see him Grandfather. I ran up to him, put my arms around him, gave him a hug and scratched him behind his ears, which he had always loved me to do."

"I asked him where he had been and what he had been doing. To my amazement, he was not happy with what I was doing and he told me to quit in a very angry, snarly bark.

Speeler told me he did not appreciate me calling him by saying "HERE Speeler! Then Speeler barked to tell me it was degrading and it was none of my business where he had been."

"Speeler told me he had a run in with Mr. Thompson when he was in his yard. He then went into the grocery store and the clerk threw him out the back door into the produce garbage in the dumpster."

"Speeler went to the fountain at City Hall to wash off and the police officer saw him and hit him with his nightstick. The police officer ran him out of the fountain and that's when Speeler went into Mr. Hanna's butcher shop and attacked Mr. Hanna and tore the leg of his pants."

"The mailman was just entering the butcher shop to deliver the morning mail. The mailman saw Mr. Hanna trying to get rid of the dog that had a hold of his pants and thinking the dog was mad and attacking Mr. Hanna, he pulled out his can of mace and sprayed Speeler in the face, just as Mr. Hanna was kicking Speeler out the door."

"At this point Speeler claims that his eyes were burning so badly that he could not see. Speeler ran out into the street attempting to make his getaway and ran in front of Homer Wallace's car. "Mr. Willacher must have attempted to avoid hitting Speeler and he crashed into a fire hydrant breaking it in two."

"Speeler then went into the alleyway across from the butcher shop and lay behind some boxes until he could at least see something. He decided to leave by the back of the alley and that is when he walked across the freshly laid concrete sidewalk at the rear of the Bishop Building. I guess the man that was laying the concrete picked up his shovel, hit Speeler in the rump with it and that Grandfather, is when Speeler ran to the park and hid under one of the bushes."

"Grandfather, that's about the time I found him and I put his leash on his collar to walk him home."

"So, you have him tied up in the back yard?" Grandfather asked.

"Well that's not the end of his problems Grandfather; there's more?"

"There is more?" Grandfather asked in disbelief.

"Yes, there is more. As we were walking home, Speeler saw Mr. and Mrs. Thompson walking down the sidewalk arm and arm. You know

Mr. Thompson has injured his leg and Mrs. Thompson was helping him to walk trying to keep him from falling."

"Yes, I knew Mr. Thompson had injured his leg; however, I did not know he was out of bed and walking."

"Well Grandfather, as we passed them on the sidewalk Speeler barked, "Hey you! 'Grumpy Old Man' why don't you and that 'Old Lady' of yours move over so someone else can walk on the sidewalk other than you."

"Of course, the Thompson did not know that my dog could talk and they naturally thought that I had said that. Grandfather, I was so embarrassed that I could not look them in the eye and tell them the truth. I am sure they would not have believed the truth anyway, so we just walked on."

"I thought it was all over and in just a few minutes we would be safe at home. I thought I could talk to you and get some advice to undo some of the cruel and spiteful things that Speeler has done today so they would never happen again."

"Speeler heard the ice cream truck coming down the street; he ran and got in the middle of the street, stopped the truck and ordered two Drumsticks. I had to pay for them with the money I was saving toward a Mother's Day gift."

"What flavor did Speeler order?" Grandfather asked."

Devo shook his head and looked at his grandfather, "Of what importance is the flavor of the ice cream, Grandfather?"

"The flavor of the ice cream has nothing to do with my story. Why do you ask, Grandfather? What difference does it make what flavor Speeler ordered?"

"I just thought it might be nice to know what Speeler's favorite flavor was so the next time I slip him some ice cream from the freezer; I will get his favorite flavor for him."

"Speeler ordered two chocolate Drumsticks, Grandfather."

"Grandfather, I think you are missing the point. I am not interested in Speeler's favorite flavor of ice cream; I am interested in what I will need to do to correct some of the things that Speeler and I did to get us in this mess."

Chapter 6

GRANDFATHER'S ADVICE

"Well, my son, Grandfather said with a great deal of affection as he placed his arm around Devo. Since you started at the beginning of your story I will start at the beginning of my story."

"After dinner last night I went into my library to decide if I should make it rain or if I should not make it rain as I told you I would do.

I looked up "RAIN" in my *Book of Magic and Incantations*. I read all the things that had to do with rain."

"Since I did not know exactly how much rain to make; I asked myself, was it one inch, was it two inches or perhaps three inches, I could only guess. Was there to be wind along with the rain? If so, how many miles per hour? Was it to be 20 miles per hour, 30 miles per hour, 50 miles per hour or even more, say 100 miles per hour? I did not know. Was there to be lightning along with the rain and wind? A lot of lightning, a little lightning, should it strike close or far away? I did not know. I finally made up my mind on the rain, the wind and the lightning and I did what I knew I had to do."

"Magic?" Devo said, "You finally arrived at the correct numbers and the correct steps indicated in your *Book of Magic and Incantations*?"

"Yes, I finally arrived at the numbers that would come with the rain, wind and lightning. I then did what I thought best; I turned out the lights and went to bed."

"Later in the night, the storm with the rain, wind and thunder came as I knew it would, I went back to sleep knowing that I had made the correct decision."

"That evening you witnessed two-and one-half inches of rain which dropped in one-and one-half hours with winds up to 60 miles per hours and a more than normal amount of electrical activity."

"When I went to the library during the storm and opened your book Grandfather, I knew you had decided to make it rain and I was so happy, it seemed to make it easier for me to make the decision to make Speeler talk."

"What you do not know Devo, is the numbers you saw written on the sheet of paper in my *Book of Magic and Incantations* were numbers that I had written down after I turned on the weather channel. You see my decision was to do nothing and to let Mother Nature take her natural course.

They had predicted severe weather for 2:00 AM until 3:30 AM. "You see I had nothing to do with the weather last night except that I did nothing to interfere with what would happen naturally."

"I knew that you had been in my book; first because I heard you go to get Speeler, later because I heard your bedroom door open, later the library door open, after that you and Speeler went down the stairs and you also spilled some candle wax on the top of my desk."

"But now on to your problem, Devo. You know that I cannot undo the magic or spell of another and you cannot undo your own spell or incantation."

"Can you help me change what I have done so that everything will be back to normal?"

"Devo, it is like what a very learned surgeon told me one time when I had my appendix removed. I asked him if I would be normal after the operation. "Sargo" he said, "A learned man like you should realize that I cannot operate on anyone and make them normal. I can only operate on them and make them better."

"You must undo this yourself; you must find a way to undo what you have done and not create a new problem. In other words, Devo you can never again make it normal but you have the ability to make it better. Think on it long and hard, then go to the library and see what needs to be done; then do it. Remember Devo, I am always here to help you."

"I will personally take care of the butcher and replace his pants. I think you will need to go to the Thompson's home and apologize to them personally. I do not believe in lying. I am sure they will be truly insulted when you try to explain that it was your dog that spoke to them. Under the circumstances I feel that omission of part of your story may be advisable; that I will leave up to you."

"Let's get started, you go to the library and do some studying and I shall go to the butcher and perhaps while I am there, I shall pick up some of that imported Salami that your mother and father like so well."

Devo went to the library and started to search in the *Book of Magic and Incantations*. He found a help section and looked up "Undo." He read; "Undo," see: Alter 345, Correct 534, Change 672, Adjust 957, Modify 1088 and Vary 2066.

After reading all the suggested help, Devo decided to do what his grandfather did; he would do nothing at the present time.

The next morning Devo went out to the dog house to feed Speeler. Speeler was excited to see him and was jumping up and down, "Where are we going, where are we going, where are we going today?"

"We're not going anywhere Speeler. You have misbehaved badly and I shall give you the same punishment that I get when I misbehave. I am sent to my room to think about what I did so that I will not do the same thing again. I shall keep you here chained to the dog house until you realize what you have done to the people around us."

"That's unfair! I did not do anything and I certainly did not misbehave, this is mean and you are very unfair and you are mistreating me badly. I want to tell...m...y....s...i...d...e....o...f....t...h...e...e...e." Devo took his hand and indicated to Speeler to zip up his lip.

Devo looked down at Speeler's doggie dish, "Whose Frisbee is this Speeler?"

"Oh, yeah! I forgot to tell you about that," Speeler barked regretfully.

"Before I left the park after the man threw his shoe at me, I turned around and ran back where the man and woman were sitting on a blanket, I grabbed his Frisbee in my mouth and ran. I ran here to my dog house set the Frisbee down beside my bowl and took a drink of water and then I went to the butcher shop," Speeler barked."

"Does it ever end?" Devo said as he turned to leave.

Devo walked back to the house and he could still hear Speeler barking until he reached the front door.

Devo sat on the front porch for a while then he went into the house, got some of his soldiers and hot wheel cars to play with. He had been playing on the porch by himself for about an hour when Grandfather opened the front door, came out on the porch and sat on the stairs.

"How are things going today Devo; have you solved your problem with Speeler?"

"Speeler is being punished Grandfather but somehow I feel I am also being punished. I have Speeler chained to the dog house so that he cannot play and roam around like he usually does. I know that is hard for him but somehow I feel that I am being punished at the same time as I do not have Speeler to play with or take walks with."

"Well, Devo think how your mother and father feel when you are sent to your room. Did you ever think that they feel badly because they do not have you by their side playing, asking questions, and telling them what you did that day or about your dreams?"

"No, Grandfather, I never thought of it that way but I shall think about that before I misbehave again and I will try to always remember the lesson I am learning from Speeler's little misadventure."

"What have you decided to do about your gift of speech to Speeler?"

"I have decided to follow your example Grandfather. I shall think about it for a while before I do anything. I see now that if I make a mistake on this spell, I shall need to cast another spell and if I make a mistake on that spell, I will need still another spell; It could go on forever."

Chapter 7

APOLOGIES

Grandfather got up and said, "I am going to see Mr. Hanna today and pay him for his damaged pants. His shop was closed yesterday so I did not get to see him. Would you like to come along with me?"

"Thank you, Grandfather I would love to walk to the butcher shop with you."

Devo and Grandfather entered the butcher shop and were greeted by a smiling Mr. Hanna.

"Good morning, Sargo and a good morning to you Devo. How is that little dog of yours today; what's his name?"

"His name is Speeler and he's not too happy as I have him chained up to the dog house."

"Well Devo, I must apologize to Speeler; I was taken by surprise when he came into the shop and I thought he talked. I believed that for a moment I was losing my mind; I know dogs do not talk. In my excitement I threw my meat tenderizer hammer at Speeler and hit the poor dog in the head."

"If I did any damage to him, I apologize and I will be more than happy to pay for any care he may need resulting from my hammer throwing. Poor thing, it's no wonder he came back and grabbed my pants; I would do the same thing if I were a dog and someone threw a meat tenderizer at me."

"I will replace your pants Mr. Hanna; I know that Speeler tore the pant leg," Devo said.

"That won't be necessary Devo, they were an old pair and I discovered that the seam in the other leg was unraveled also so I threw them away."

"Now what can I do for you Mr. Mannix?"

"I would like six slices of Garlic Baloney cut very thick and three-quarter pounds of your best imported Salami."

Devo and his grandfather left the butcher shop and started for home with the package of Garlic Baloney and the imported Salami.

"Grandfather, it seemed to me that you knew Mr. Hanna would not make us replace his pants."

"Devo, I have known Mr. Hanna for over thirty years now and I know him to be a just and honorable man. I thought if given enough time he might see what happened between him and Speeler in a different light. My faith in him was justified."

"Do you feel up to stopping at the Thompson's to apologize for Speeler?"

"That would be nice Grandfather; I have been worried about what I would say to them all morning."

"Good morning, Mildred, Devo and I just stopped over to see how Herald was getting along. We heard he had a fall and had injured his leg."

"Good morning, Sago, it's good to see you and Devo; we have only been out of the house once since Herald's accident; and since I am thinking about its Devo, I want to apologize for taking up the whole sidewalk yesterday. I was having such a terrible time with Herald; he was in so much pain that I got impatient with him and lost my temper. Will you accept my apology, Devo?"

"Yes, I certainly do Mrs. Thompson and I need to apologize to you and Mr. Thompson. I, also, was having a terrible day and everything was going wrong, I think my dog and I were losing our temper and some things were said that I truly regret."

"Well thank you Devo. You are really a well-mannered, sweet, young man. I shall tell your mother the next time I see her at bridge, what a nice young man you are."

"Let's go into the parlor and see Herald; I think he may be asleep but I will wake him up if he is."

When Grandfather and Devo entered the parlor, Herald sat up in his chair and said, "Sargo, it is great to see you; I have not seen you since my accident almost a month ago, how have you been?"

"I have been fine Herald; how is that leg of yours coming along?"

"Well I have good days and I have bad days; yesterday was a bad day and I was in a lot of pain. I think I took my suffering out on your poor little dog, Speeler. He was in the front yard and I threw my morning newspaper at him. There was really no call for me to do such an unkind act; later I thought I should control my temper and not take my problem out on other people."

"Mr. Thompson, I never let Speeler out by himself, I always have him on a leash but he stayed the night with me during the storm; I was scared by the lightning and thunder so he slept with me. I think Speeler got out in the morning when Dad went to work. If Speeler did any harm to your yard I will fix it and I do apologize on his behalf," Devo said.

"Thank you, Devo, it is kind of you to offer, but no damage was done. What brings you out so early this morning, Sargo?"

"I heard you were up and about but still not walking very good so I stopped to see Karl at the butcher shop to get you a little get well present."

Sargo handed Mr. Thompson the package of Garlic Baloney and said, "You may have to share that with your wife, Herald."

'Thank you so much Sargo, you know it's my favorite; and as for sharing I may let Mildred have one slice, but no more."

"Well, Herald it's nice to see you up and about again. Devo and I have a busy day today and we need to get going."

As they started to leave Herald said, "Hey Sargo, did you have anything to do with the storm the other day?"

"Sorry Herald I would like to take the credit but I am innocent."

Chapter 8

THE INCANTATION

A week had passed and Speeler was still chained to the dog house. Devo had just walked up with a clean dish of water and a dish of doggie food when Speeler came out of his house and sat down in front of Devo.

"Devo, I have been thinking and I have thought over what happened that caused me to be chained to my dog house. I realize that I was so excited about being able to hear, understand and speak to people that I got carried away with my enthusiasm. I realize that I probably got you in a lot of trouble and at the time; I did not care. I do care now; you are my best friend and you deserve more than the misery and pain that I brought you. Will you accept my apology?"

Devo bent over and unhooked Speeler's chain and placed the leash on his collar.

"Want to go for a walk?"

"I take that as a yes for accepting my apology," Speeler barked.

"There are a few things we need to do before I accept your apology Speeler. I will pick up that Frisbee and we will be on our way," Devo said.

Devo took Speeler to the house and went into the library; Devo opened the *Book of Magic and Incantations*.

Devo opened the book to the page marked "UNDERSTANDING."

Devo sat Speeler in a chair close to the desk and said, "I believe making you talk was a mistake Speeler as it only got both of us in trouble. Grandfather tells me that I cannot change what I did so I must cast another spell to attempt to correct my first spell. When I am through you will still be able to speak and understand my language."

"My teacher at school thinks that I lead a life that is more exciting than most of the other children in the class. She thinks that someday I should become a writer and tell everyone of my childhood adventures with my dog Speeler. I shall give that serious consideration as I grow up Speeler."

"If I ever write a story of my adventures with my talking dog Speeler; as my teacher suggested; then and only then, will the children who read my story be able to hear and understand you."

"You must be aware that until then no one will understand you except me, all they will hear are your barks. I advise you not to do a lot of barking as it may become annoying and I will need to chain you to the dog house until you promise not to bark too much. Do you fully understand, Speeler?"

"Yes, Devo," I understand and thank you. I want you to know that you are my best friend and I shall always love you."

"Now back to your spell Speeler. I have decided that since I cannot undo my spell, I shall make a few minor adjustments to it."

Devo read the following directions from the *Book of Magic and Incantations.*

The one who is to perform the incantation will need the following items.

One white triangle, one circle that fits inside the triangle, three candles and something from the subject that the incantation is to be applied too.

Devo took two sheets of paper from the computer's printer. He cut one into a triangle and one into a circle that fit within the triangle.

Devo placed the triangle on his grandfather's desk, put a candle on each point and lit them.

Reading on in the *Book of Magic and Incantations*, it said: Write, '*Understanding*' on the circle seven times. Place the circle on the subject briefly and then place it in the center of the triangle. Place the item that you have selected from the subject in the center of the circle.

Devo went over to Speeler and brushed four hairs from his back. He placed the hairs on the circle.

Devo read on; There are four things that the Conjurer must do to cast this spell on the subject:

While stating your request the subjects head should be at eye level of the Conjurer. Look the subject in the eye while you are expressing your proposal.

Devo stood in front of Speeler and looked him straight in the eye and said, "When my dog Speeler speaks everyone in the universe except me will hear only his bark, I alone shall hear and understand what he is saying," Devo said in a whispered voice.

1. While the Conjurer cups one hands over the mouth of the subject, call upon Erebos, The God of darkness and shadows, asking to have the requested incantation allowed.

2. "Oh! Erebos, God of darkness and shadows, I beseech you to grant my request that I be the only human who can understand Speeler's barking, except, for anyone who reads my book explaining how I came to cast this spell."

   While the Conjurer cups both hands over the ears of the subject call upon Tartarus the God of the deepest, darkest part of the underworld, asking to have the requested incantation allowed.

   "Oh! Tartarus the God of the deepest, darkest part of the underworld, I beseech you to grant my request that I be the only human who can understand Speeler's barking, except, for anyone who reads my book explaining how I came to cast this spell."

3. The Conjurer must tap the head of the subject seven times while saying "Erebos and Tartarus, I command you to fulfill my wishes."

* Caution this spell cannot be undone. The spell that you have cast will last forever in the subject's lifetime.

Devo performed the four tasks that the spell required and then he went over to Speeler and while looking him in the eye, he placed his hands on Speeler's mouth, then on his head and said, "Oh, Erebos and Tartarus, I command you to fulfill my wishes, Oh! Erebos and Tartarus I command you to fulfill my wishes." Devo said the magic words the required seven times as set forth in Grandfather's *Book of Magic and Incantations*."

For one brief moment, Speeler was surrounded with a halo of green iridescent light. Speeler gave an involuntary quiver and then he looked at Devo and said, "Man that was eerie."

Speeler looked up at Devo and said, "I'm feeling hungry do you suppose you could fix me a wiener or some lunch meat?"

Chapter 9

FORGIVENESS

"**C**ome on Speeler, we have a few more things to do before I accept your apology. I will pick up the Frisbee and we will be on our way."

Devo put the leash on Speeler and they walked to Mr. Hanna's butcher shop.

"Good morning Mr. Hanna," Devo said.

"Good morning Devo, I see you have brought Speeler back to see me," Mr. Hanna said.

"Well, Speeler, I certainly do want to apologize for throwing my meat tenderizer hammer at you the other day. I was so stunned when I thought you talked; I sort of lost control."

"And I am sorry for ripping your pants, Mr. Hanna," Speeler barked. "That's really a smart dog you have there Devo. He seems to know what I am saying and I could almost swear he answered me back."

Mr. Hanna came out from behind the meat counter knelt down and patted Speeler on the head. "There, there," Mr. Hanna said as he patted Speeler on the head, "I just want to make sure you and I are friends again Speeler. I have a nice bone for you back in the scrap barrel in the refrigerator. You wait right here and I'll get it for you. It will sort of be my peace offering," Mr. Hanna said.

Mr. Hanna went into the meat locker, took one of his bones and gave it to Speeler.

"I hope that Frisbee isn't for me, Devo, Mr. Hanna said. I'm too old to run after a Frisbee and I don't have a dog."

"No Mr. Hanna, I found this Frisbee lying next to Speeler's water bowl and I want to see if I can return it to the owner," Devo said.

"Mr. Hanna do you know what ever happened to the mail that Mr. Kinkel lost in the street yesterday when he dropped his mailbag?" Devo asked.

"Well, as a matter of fact, I do Devo. When the police and fire department arrived here, they all helped Mr. Kinkel retrieve his mail. Arnie took all the mail back to the post office let it dry overnight and I think he is delivering it today. I don't think he lost a single letter," Mr. Hana said.

"And what about Mr. Willacher and the busted fire hydrant; whatever happened there?" Devo asked.

"Well the police found out that Homer Willacher was driving while putting on a pair of old socks and looking at a map at the same time. He was trying to find the Law Offices of Mannix, Littman and Kincaid when the accident occurred. It seems Mr. Willacher was cited by the police in Maineville last Friday night for this exact same offense and he needed an attorney to accompany him to Mayor's Court when his case comes up."

"I went out in the street right after the accident to see if I could assist Homer in case he was injured. I said to him, "You know you almost hit that little dog, Homer?"

"Homer looked at me and said, "What dog, I didn't see any dog."

"Thank you so much for the information Mr. Hanna. I am so happy that Mr. Willacher was not injured and that the mailman recovered all of his mail," Devo said.

Speeler barked his thanks to Mr. Hana, said goodbye, picked up his bone and headed toward the door.

Devo said goodbye to Mr. Hanna and the two of them left the butcher shop. As they walked down the street, Speeler stopped and laid his bone down on the sidewalk.

"Well, that wasn't too bad, Speeler barked. "I thought Mr. Hanna might throw the meat cleaver at me when I returned; instead that nice old man gave me a bone."

"Where to next, Devo?" Speeler barked.

"I thought we would go to the park to see if we can find the owner of this Frisbee," Devo said.

When Speeler and Devo entered the park, Speeler barked, "I think that's the same couple sitting over there on that park bench."

Devo and Speeler walked over to the park bench and when they got close, the woman seated on the bench said, "Andrew, I think that is the little dog that took our Frisbee,"

"Before the man or woman could say anything more to Devo and Speeler, Devo reached out with the Frisbee and said, "I believe this belongs to you. I am so sorry; I think my dog might have taken it from you and I want to return it."

"Is that your dog?" the man asked.

"Yes Sir, he is," Devo replied.

"I didn't know he had an owner, I thought he was just a stray dog and I was afraid he might attack me or my friend."

"The poor thing, I threw my shoe at him because I think stray dogs cannot be trusted. Sometimes they come from places where they have been abused and they tend to become very mean. I thought he might attack us. I can see now that he is a well-mannered, cared for dog."

"If this is your Frisbee, I do want to apologize for my dog taking it. Tell the man you are sorry, Speeler."

Speeler sat in front of the man raised his right paw and barked, "Sorry I took your Frisbee."

"He really is a cute dog and the next time you two are in the park, if you want to play Frisbee with me, just come over and I'll play a few rounds with you," the man said.

"Incidentally, my name is Andrew Carlson and my friend is Margaret Taylor."

"I am glad to meet you Mr. Carlson and Ms. Taylor, my name is Devo Mannix and this is my dog Speeler."

Mr. Carlson reached out and shook Devo's hand then he bent over and patted Speeler on the head.

"I know Speeler would love to play with you and the Frisbee but right now he has a bone from Mr. Hanna the butcher and he needs to take it home," Devo said.

"We will play another day Speeler. You come back and get me," Mr. Carlson said.

"What's next on our list of things to do," Speeler barked.

"I plan to take you home so you can put your bone in your doggie dish then we shall go to see Mr. and Mrs. Thompson. You will need to give them an apology also," Devo said.

When they reached home, Speeler put his bone down, took a drink from his doggie bowl and asked Devo if he could have about 10 minutes to chew on his new bone.

"I'll give you 10 minutes then I want you to take me to where they were pouring the cement sidewalk so we can see how much damage you did and then we will go to Mr. and Mrs. Thompson's home," Devo said.

Speeler took Devo through the woods, past Lowbrook's Pond, down Taylor Street, through the backyard of one of the houses and they ended up at the rear of the Bishop Building.

The cement was still fresh but it was dry enough now that one could probably walk on it. Devo examined the sidewalk and much to his amazement he saw embedded in the cement, six handprints, two paw prints, in addition to Speeler's paw prints where he ran across the sidewalk.

Above the handprints, the words Sarah, Maggie and Annie were written into the cement. Above the two paw prints was written the word, Cotton.

"Looks like someone else has added graffiti to the sidewalk, Speeler," Devo said.

Devo and Speeler walked around to the front of the Bishop Building and went in the front door.

"Is Mr. Bishop here, please?" Devo asked.

"I am Mr. Bishop; how can I help you?"

"Mr. Bishop, I think my dog ran through the wet cement on your sidewalk yesterday and left his paw prints."

"Oh yes! I saw them. The cement finishers were very angry and I think one of them hit your poor dog with his shovel.

"He called me out to look at the damage and when I saw the paw prints in the cement, I was so impressed that I had my wife bring my three daughters over to the store."

"My daughters put their handprints and wrote their names in the wet cement. They brought their cat with them and they had Cotton put his paws in the cement also."

"Can I do anything to repay you for the damage to your sidewalk that my dog Speeler did Mr. Bishop?" Devo asked.

"Repay me for damages? Oh, no Devo. I need to thank Speeler for his great idea of putting footprints in the sidewalk. I shall have a memorial to my daughter's hands and Cotton's paws in my sidewalk for the rest of my life. Some day when they have left home and I am missing them I can come out the back door of my building and remember the happy day and the fun we had putting their hands in the cement," Mr. Bishop said tearfully.

Mr. Bishop thanked Devo and Speeler once again and rewarded them each with a candy bar for stopping to talk to him.

"Where to now, Devo?" Speeler barked.

"We are going to the Thompson's," Devo said.

Devo took Speeler to the Thompson house and asked to see Mr. Thompson.

Mrs. Thompson took Speeler and Devo out on the back porch were Mr. Thompson was sitting with his leg propped up on a pillow as he drank his morning coffee.

"Good morning Mr. Thompson, how is your leg today?"

"It's much better, Devo. I'm seeing a little improvement in it every day. What brings you to our house today, Devo?"

"I came over to apologize to you and Mrs. Thompson for my behavior the other day. My dog and I were in a very bad mood as we were having an extremely bad day," Devo said.

Speeler walked over to Mr. Thompson and licked his hand.

"I am very sorry Mr. and Mrs. Thompson for the mean things I said to you the other day," Speeler barked.

Mr. Thompson patted Speeler on the head when he heard Speeler bark, he said, "Mildred, why don't you go to the kitchen and get this nice dog a piece of my Garlic Baloney. I think I shall share a slice with him."

As Speeler and Devo walked home, Speeler stopped briefly and ate his slice of Garlic Baloney.

Speeler looked up at Devo and barked, "I have found that apologizing for my misbehaving has been most rewarding. I have a great bone that I can chew on all day, a candy bar and that tasty slice of thick Garlic Baloney, but more than that, I feel good inside for apologizing for the mistakes I made."

"Speeler, since you ate your slice of Garlic Baloney and are sitting in the middle of the sidewalk looking up at me, I would imagine you want to know if I accept your apology."

"That would be nice, Speeler barked as he sat with his right paw raised for a handshake in case Devo forgave him.

Devo reached down and shook Speeler's paw and Speeler took the opportunity to give Devo a lick on the cheek.

"Speeler, I think we both have learned a lot from our mistakes and I will now accept your apology, but please don't lick my face again when you have been eating Garlic Baloney."

Chapter 10

GONE FISHING

It was a beautiful morning in Brown County and Devo had just walked on to the front porch to look for Speeler. Of course, When Speeler saw Devo on the front porch; he stood up in front of his dog house and ran to the front porch to be by Devo's side.

Devo heard the screen door close behind him and he turned to see his grandfather walking out onto the porch with a cup of coffee in his hand.

"Good morning, Grandfather, how are you feeling this morning?" Devo asked.

"I feel great this morning, Grandfather said, I just came out on the porch to join you to enjoy this beautiful morning."

"How are you feeling this morning, Devo?"

"Well Grandfather to tell the truth I am still upset with my teacher for giving me a "C" on my math test when all the answers were correct," Devo said.

"Why did your teacher give you a "C" when all the answers were correct?" Grandfather asked.

"She said I had all the answers correct but I did not follow her instructions. Then she gave me a lecture on following the rules," Devo told his grandfather.

"Well look at it this way, Devo if none of the players in a baseball game followed the rules there would be a lot of confusion and no one would enjoy playing," Grandfather said.

"I see what you mean Grandfather, I will keep that in mind," Devo said.

"What would you like to do today, Speeler?" Devo asked his dog.

"It's a beautiful morning Devo, what say you and I go fishing at Lowbrook's Pond, that way I could have a fish sandwich for lunch," Speeler barked.

"I have never been fishing, Speeler? That may be a lot of fun."

"Piece of cake, Devo, I know all there is to know about fishing, I saw this guy on TV doing it and it is really easy it was called *Fishing with Fred*." Just then, Sargo Mannix, Devo's Grandfather stood up and started to walk into the yard.

Sargo was by far the most notable and respected sorcerer in all of America and possibly of the world and Devo was studying to be his apprentice.

"What are you and Speeler planning to do today?" Grandfather asked. "We were just talking about going fishing at Lowbrook's Pond," Devo said.

"Have you ever gone fishing before?" Grandfather asked.

"No Grandfather, but Speeler saw this man on TV do a lot of fishing and he really catches some big fish," Devo said.

"Speeler told me he knows what to do," Devo said.

"Well there is just a little more to being a good fisherman then seeing it done on TV. I would be happy to go with you and Speeler and share some of my experience and know-how about fishing if you would like."

"We don't need your grandfather's advice, Devo, I know what I am doing and I can tell you everything about fishing that you will need to know," Speeler remarked.

"What did Speeler say Devo?" Grandfather asked.

"He said to tell you thanks but he thinks we can handle this one alone."

"Well, I plan to go to town later this morning but if you need any help, just call me when I get back home."

"Come on Devo, you and I will go to the tool shed to see if we can find a pole and some string; then we will go to the house and look for something in the refrigerator to use for bait. If I am lucky, I may find some leftovers to eat," Speeler barked.

Devo and Speeler walked to the tool shed, opened the door and looked to see what they could find in the way of equipment to begin their fishing trip to Lowbrook's Pond.

"I see some kite string up on the top shelf, Devo, I am sure we can use that for our fishing line," Speeler barked.

"That's great Speeler; now let's look for a pole to tie the string to." Devo and Speeler searched the entire tool shed but they could not come up with a suitable pole to use.

"I saw a fisherman in Africa on the TV show Fishing with Fred that did not have a fishing pole, so he tied his string to his big toe. That way you could lie down on your back, look up at the clouds and imagine all sort of strange things formed by the clouds; people's faces, dragons, fish and all sort of bizarre animals. I know you love to do that. You can even go to sleep if there are no clouds or you get bored," Speeler barked.

"If you get a bite, the fish would pull on your big toe and wake you up, if you happen to have fallen asleep. I think that will work well for you," Speeler barked.

"You want to tie the fishing line to my big toe?" Devo asked.

"I hope you're not thinking of tying the string to my toe, Speeler barked. My toes are so small it would be hard to tie a knot around one of them. Besides, I don't want to sit all day waiting for a bite, I want to sniff around in the woods and along the pond to see if there's anything I can eat."

"Are you always hungry Speeler?"

"Yeah,......most of the time," Speeler barked.

"I thought you wanted to go fishing?" Devo said.

"Well, yeah, but fishing for a dog is a lot different than human fishing, I do a lot of running and chasing along with a whole bunch of sniffing. I might even find Squirrel and chase him up a tree. Boy what fun that will be. I am excited about our fishing trip already," Speeler barked.

"Let's go to the house and look in the refrigerator and see what we can find to use for bait."

Chapter 11

TO CATCH A FISH

evo and Speeler walked to the house and went to the kitchen. Speeler barked, "Fish like shrimp and steak. Let's look in the freezer and see if we can find something like that."

Devo placed all the frozen bags of food on the kitchen table. He was hoping to find something like shrimp to use for bait, as Speeler had suggested.

The only thing that Devo could find that Speeler mentioned for fish bait beside the shrimp was steak.

His mother had frozen the eight steaks she purchased for the family Fourth of July party.

"There will only be six of you at the party so I am sure your mom will not miss one of the steaks," Speeler barked.

After he replaced all of frozen food in the freezer; Devo took one of the frozen steaks to his bedroom and put it in his backpack along with the kite string.

"I will need something for a fishhook Speeler, do you have any ideas?"

"How about a paperclip, I think that would make a swell fishhook."

"You are so smart Speeler, Devo said, I sure hope there are fish in Lowbrook's Pond.

"Speeler, I have never seen anyone fishing in Lowbrook's Pond before. Are you sure there are fish in there?"

"Can't say, don't know," Speeler barked, as he sniffed Devo's backpack to see if there was anything he could find to eat.

"I think I would like to do an incantation to make sure there are fish in Lowbrook's Pond before we go out and sit on the bank all day." Devo said as he watched Speeler sniff around his backpack, looking for food.

"Do you think there's fish in the pond?" Speeler asked.

"Gee, I don't know Speeler but I do know how to make sure there are some; let's take a look at Grandfather's *Book of Magic and Incantations* and see what it has to offer," Devo said.

Devo picked up his backpack put it on his back and headed for Grandfather's library. When they arrived, Devo turned on the desk lamp and opened up Grandfather's *Book of Magic and Incantations*.

Devo knew that his grandfather had warned him not to use The *Book of Magic and Incantations* without him being present in the room so that he could guide Devo in its use.

"Do you think it will be all right if I use Grandfather's *Book of Magic and Incantations*? Devo asked Speeler, hoping to get support from his dog for what he was about to do.

"I think it will be all right for you to use it just once without Grandfather's help. After all you are just going to put a few fish in Lowbrook's Pond." Speeler barked.

"I am sure you will be all right, considering we are only dealing with a few fish here; nothing really important. Besides, you do want to be sure there are fish in Lowbrook's Pond, don't you?" Speeler barked.

Devo opened the big leather-bound book and turned to the page that was marked "Fish."

Under the title *"Fish"* Devo found the subtitle called "Stocking Fish" Devo read the incantation and went about gathering the things necessary items to perform the spell.

A. To perform the incantation, you will need three candles, triangular shaped white cloth, a white circle of cloth that will fit within the triangle, three lighted candles, a live fish or an epitome of the fish to be produced, a container filled with water and the use of a magic wand.

"What is an epitome?" Speeler barked.

"I do not know but I can look it up in the index, Speeler."

"Let's see, epigram, epilogue, episode, and epitome; a person or thing that is typical of or possesses to a high degree the features of a whole class: The wolf is the epitome of a dog.

I guess that means the dog looks like a wolf," Devo said.

"Sounds right, Speeler barked. Now all we need to do is find something which has the features of a whole class of fish."

"If we had an aquarium, we could use that," Devo said.

Devo and Speeler went to the dining room and carried three battery-operated candles into Grandfather's library. Devo was not allowed to use matches because the last time he used them in Grandfather's den he got candle wax all over the top of the desk.

"I think the battery-operated candles will work just fine," Devo said. Devo took two pieces of white printer paper from the computer's printer, since he did not have any white cloth.

Devo removed a ruler from the top drawer of grandfather's desk to measure out an equilateral triangle. Using the ruler Devo had laid out four or five different triangles and then erase each of them with the pencil eraser.

"What are you trying to do?" Speeler barked, as he sat on the desk looking down at Devo's drawing.

"I am trying to make an equilateral triangle," Devo said as he intently drew another triangle.

"What is an equilateral triangle?" Speeler barked.

"For your information Mr. Speeler. It is a triangle that has three equal sides," Devo said.

"You are so smart; wherever did you learn that?" Speeler barked.

"My mother explained that to me when she was making patches for a bed quilt. It had thousands of equilateral triangles of all different colors sewn into one great center design." Devo said.

"Interesting," Speeler barked.

After a few more tries Devo finally cut out an equilateral triangle. Devo took the triangle to the kitchen and laid it on the counter. He removed several size cans from the pantry and laid them on the triangle to see which one would fit best. After several attempts Devo found a can of shredded chicken breast, which fit exactly in the center of the triangle. He placed the can of shredded chicken breast on a sheet of white printer paper and drew a circle using the bottom of the can as a guide.

Devo returned to Grandfather den, cut out the circle, and placed it alongside the equilateral triangle.

Next, the directions instructed that Devo. Was to place one lighted candle at each point of the triangle.

Following the instructions, Devo inscribe the words "Provide" and "Fish" on the round circle seven times. Devo placed the triangle on his grandfather's desk and placed one lighted battery-operated candles on each point of the triangle.

Devo read on:

There are seven things that the Conjurer must do to cast the spell for the production of fish.

1. The Conjurer must state his intention.
2. The fish or epitome should be at eye level of the Conjurer.
3. Look at the fish or epitome while you are performing the incantation.
4. The Conjurer shall place the round circle with the words "Provide" and "Fish," briefly on the fish or epitome, Place the container filled with water in the center of the circle. Place the fish or epitome on top of the vessel containing the water.
5. The Conjurer shall cup both hands over the container of water while calling upon Erebos, the God of darkness, asking him to place an adequate amount of fish at the Conjurer's selected location.
6. The Conjurer shall cup both hands above each candle while calling upon Tartarus the God of shadows, asking him to have the incantation granted.
7. The Conjurer must tap the fish or epitome seven times while saying Erebos and Tartarus I command you to fulfill my wishes.

* Caution this spell cannot be undone. The fish or epitome shall appear in the place designated by the Conjurer.

Chapter 12

BAITING THE HOOK

Devo and Speeler went to the basement, took a Mason jar and filled it with water; they took it to the library and placed it on Grandfather's desk along with the candles.

"Speeler we do not have a fish to show as an example for our spell; do you have any ideas what we can do?"

"How about a picture of a fish. That is a thing that is typical of or possesses to a high degree the features of a whole class?" Speeler barked.

"That might work Speeler, where can we get a picture of a fish?"

"How about looking in one of the copies of National Geographic Magazine?" Speeler barked.

"Great idea Speeler, let's go to the living room and look through some of the magazines there."

Devo and Speeler went to the living room and the two of them looked at all the new magazines, searching for pictures of fish.

"Look here Devo, I found a picture of an Orca; do you think that will work?" Speeler barked excitedly."

A fish is a fish, is a fish, Speeler; let's tear it out and use it," Devo said.

Devo tore the picture of the Orca from the magazine and they returned to Grandfather's den to arrange all the items for the incantation.

Devo placed three battery-operated candles on each point of the triangle and placed the Mason jar filled with water in the center of the circle. They placed the picture of the Orca on the lid of the jar and turned on the candles.

Devo removed his grandfather's magic wand from the case and held it in his right hand.

First Devo had to make his wish known so he said, "I wish for a big fish in Lowbrook's Pond that I can catch."

Devo was now ready to perform the five tasks that the spell required. He went over to the desk and while looking at the Mason jar and the picture from National Geographic magazine, he placed his hands on the Orca epitome.

Devo said, "Oh Erebos and Tartarus, I command you to fulfill my wishes, Oh! Erebos and Tartarus, I command you to fulfill my wishes."

Devo said the magic words the required seven times as set forth in Grandfather's *Book of Magic and Incantations.*

For one brief moment, the vessel of water with the Orca epitome was surrounded with a halo of green shimmery light.

Devo then waved his grandfather's magic wand and recited the words necessary to cast the spell that he had copied from the *Book of Magic and Incantations.*

"From the candles, take the fire.

Grant the wish that I desire.

In the center, I have laid.

Epitome to fish; I want to trade.

Devo repeated the incantation seven times.

When they were finished, they turned off the candles, returned the candles to the dining room, the Mason jar to the basement and tossed the epitome on Devo's footlocker.

"Well we know there will be big fish in the pond Speeler; I sure hope they are biting," Devo said.

Devo and Speeler walked down the gravel road and through the woods to the banks of Lowbrook's Pond.

Devo removed the kite string, the frozen steak and the paper clip from his backpack.

"Will I need to unwrap the steak?" Devo asked.

"No, just make a hook out of the paper clip attach one end of it to the wrapping paper on the steak and throw the hook and bait to the middle of the pond in the deep water if you can," Speeler barked as he went sniffing along the edge of the pond.

"The deep water is where the big fish hide," Speeler barked.

Devo did as instructed by his mentor, throwing the frozen steak almost to the center of the pond.

"Good job, Devo; now break the string about three feet longer than you need it to be and tie it to your big toe. Now just stay there until you feel a tug on your toe and then reel your fish in. It is so simple I am sure you can handle it from here Devo. I am going to see if I can find my friend Squirrel and play Chase.

"Don't you want to stay and watch me catch my fish, Speeler?"

"Nah, I have better things to do, I am going to sniff around the edge of the pond and see what I can find that is interesting," Speeler barked.

"See you later Pal, I'm going to lay down here in the grass by the side of the pond and watch the clouds. I love to use my imagination to see what I can discover in the shape formed by the clouds.

Chapter 13

LOWBROOK'S POND

"Look, see that big cloud over there looks like a dragon's head and that one just below it looks like an old man sleeping on his back." Devo said to no one in particular.

It was so quiet and peaceful and the only thing Devo could hear was the far-off barking of Speeler who was saying, "I will catch you; I will catch you; I will catch you."

Devo soon fell asleep and he had just started to dream about driving his father's car in a race at the Indianapolis 500 Speedway, when he was suddenly awakened by something pulling very hard on his big toe. He thought for a moment that he would be dragged into the pond.

Devo dug his heels into the wet mud; he thought for sure that whatever was on his fishing line would pull off his toe.

Devo closed his eyes, turned over on his stomach, clawed in the mud with his fingers and dug his toes in to the muddy shoreline until he was sure he was far enough from the water's edge that he could not be pulled into the pond.

When the pulling on Devo's toes stopped, Devo opened his eyes and rolled over on his back. There lying at the edge of the pond in the shallow water was an Orca whale. It was the biggest fish Devo had ever seen in his life.

<< Insert Photo>>

It Was The Biggest Fish Devo Had Ever Seen

With a booming loud swish, the Orca shot a fountain of mist soaring into the air from its blowhole! The mist fell on Devo wetting all of his clothes.

"Speeler, Speeler, Speeler, come and help me; I caught a fish and I don't know what to do next," Devo said.

"I can't come right now, I have Squirrel trapped in the tree and I am pretty sure I can catch him today," Speeler barked.

"Speeler, what's the most important thing right now, me or Squirrel?"

There was a long pause of silence and Devo called again, "Speeler, did you hear me?"

Finally, Speeler Barked, "I'm thinking."

"You are thinking? What are you thinking about?" Devo called.

"I'm trying to decide what is the most important thing, coming to help you or catching Squirrel," Speeler barked.

"Fine friend you turned out to be, Speeler."

"I'm coming; I'm coming, hold your horses."

Speeler came running through the underbrush and ran up to Devo who was still sitting on the shoreline with the string tied to his big toe. "Wow! That's the biggest fish I ever saw," Speeler barked.

"Me too Speeler; whatever will I do with him?"

"I know we cannot carry him home," Speeler barked.

"We can't leave him here, Speeler. A big fish like that cannot live in a little pond like this very long. Do you have any suggestions, Speeler? It wasn't too long ago that you were bragging about what a great fisherman you are," Devo said.

"I didn't know you were going to catch a whale," Speeler barked. "Neither did I," Devo said.

"I do have an idea though, why don't we ask your grandfather what to do, he always seems to know a lot about things like this."

"That's a great idea Speeler; lets you and I go home and talk to Grandfather."

Devo untied the kite string from his big toe; then he headed home with Speeler.

When Speeler and Devo reached the house, Grandfather was sitting on the front porch whittling on a stick with his pocketknife. "What was all the barking about Devo?"

"Oh, that was Speeler, Grandfather. He had Squirrel up a tree and was having the time of his life barking," Devo said.

"What were you boys up to this morning, did you go fishing?"

"I went fishing Grandfather, Speeler decided to play Chase with Squirrels."

"Did you catch anything?" Grandfather asked.

"I did get one bite, Grandfather; Speeler did not catch anything."

"Did you bring your catch home?" Grandfather asked.

"No Grandfather, it is still down at the pond."

"Did you throw the fish back in the pond?"

"No Grandfather, it is still tied to my line. I haven't quite decided what to do with it," Devo said.

"Grandfather, while I was sitting there on the bank of the pond looking up at the sky, a thought suddenly came to my mind and I need your help to solve my problem."

"Tell me what your problem is Devo and I will see if I can help you," Grandfather said.

"I was thinking, Grandfather if a person had a really big objects and if it were not in it's proper place, and it weighed so much that the person could not carry it or lift it. What if it had to be moved or it would cause a terrible problem; what would you do?" Devo asked his grandfather.

"Can you tell me what the object is, Devo?" Grandfather asked.

"I was thinking that it might be something like a gigantic boulder sitting on top of a hill and it was about to roll down the hill into the houses below causing a lot of damage. Is there something you could do?" Devo asked. Devo asked.

Chapter 14

ADVICE FROM GRANDFATHER

"Why don't you just tell your grandfather you caught a whale?" Speeler barked.

"What is Speeler barking about?" Grandfather asked.

"I think he's just anxious to get back and chase Squirrel again," Devo said.

"Well in answer to your question Devo, there is a way to move large objects so that they will no longer pose a threat. You could use a magical incantation and turn the rocks into gravel or sand.

The whole process is very difficult and if not properly performed could cause catastrophic results," Grandfather said.

"I do want you to remember Devo if you made that rock by an incantation then it cannot be undone. Of course, it depends on what you said when you were performing the magic.

"Let me give you an example Devo. If you created this large rock and said in your incantation something like "I want a large rock on top of White Rock Mountain; that large rock will always be on White Rock Mountain as long as it is a rock. Of course, you could try pictorial transportation," Grandfather said.

"What is pictorial transportation?" Devo asked.

"In the example that you gave me you could take a picture of the rock to be moved and using a magical incantation you could move it to a safer place on top of White Rock Mountain," Grandfather said.

"Thank you, Grandfather, I think you have answered my questions. Tell Mom, Speeler and I went back to Lowbrook's Pond to finish fishing and squirrel chasing," Devo said.

Devo and Speeler left Grandfather sitting on the porch and walked back to Lowbrook's Pond.

"So, what are you going to do?" Speeler barked. I don't see how anything Grandfather told you is going to be of help, Devo. I think you're right back where we started."

"Ah, my fine furry friend, if you had listened closely you would have heard Grandfather say, "A large rock will always be on White Rock Mountain as long as it is a rock," now suppose our Orca whales is not a whale, let us suppose that it is now a single pig. What would you think of that Speeler?"

"Why not make it a squirrel and then I would have two squirrels to chase?" Speeler barked.

"You can't even catch one squirrel, Speeler. Besides, what are you going to do when you catch Squirrel?"

"Gee, Devo, I really haven't thought that far ahead," Speeler barked as he scratched the side of his head with his paw.

"But what about the part in the incantation directions where it said this spell could not be undone. What are you going to do about that?" Speeler barked.

"Well if you were listening very carefully when I cast this incantation, I said, "I wish for a big fish in Lowbrook's Pond that I can catch."

The fish was in Lowbrook's Pond and I caught it. The terms of the incantation have been met so that now nothing remains to be fulfilled," Devo said.

"Let's go back to the pond; I will check my Orca and you can check on Squirrel. Then we will go home and wait for Grandfather to drive to town," Devo said.

Devo's, Orca had let go of the frozen steak and was now swimming in the deepest part of the pond.

When Speeler got back to the pond, Devo asked him what happened to his friend, Squirrel.

"Squirrel chattered he was tired of playing Chase. He picked up a Walnut and then he went back to his nest to eat lunch.

It was about 11 o'clock before Grandfather left the house in his car.

As soon as he was out of the driveway, Devo and Speeler went to Grandfather's den and opened his *Book of Magic and Incantations.*

"What are we looking for?" Speeler barked.

"I'm looking for something that will change something into something else," Devo said.

"I' would look in the index under change," Speeler barked.

"Let's...s..e...e," Devo mumbled; there is alteration, modification, variation, conversion, adjustment. I think conversion best suits our needs. Ah, it says see; Changing, arrangement, shape, appearance, structure, looks, variety, kind and form," Devo said as he turned the pages of the book.

"What do you think, Speeler?"

"Well what do I know, I'm just your dog; however, if I were making the choice, I would choose variety."

"Why would you choose variety," Devo asked.

"Well changing its shape, appearance or looks does not seem to fit. It would still be an Orca and it would still need to be in Lowbrook's Pond. If we change its variety from a fish to a pig; it would be closer to what we need to do," Speeler barked.

Chapter 15

AN INCANTATION

"**O**kay Speeler let's see what variety says."

Devo went to the page marked "variety" and read the incantation very carefully. He took a pencil and paper from his grandfather's desk and made a few notes. Devo closed the book and told Speeler they had a lot of work to do collecting the necessary items for the incantation.

After Speeler and Devo had gathered everything necessary to change the Orcas to a pig, they assembled everything on the top of Grandfather's desk.

Devo and Speeler had collected all the necessary items with the exception of the hair from the back of a pig.

"We do not have a hair from the back of a pig. There are no pigs on any of our neighbor's farms, Devo said, do you have any suggestions Speeler?"

"The only thing I can think of is the jar of pickled pig's feet that your mother has in the pantry," Speeler barked.

"Great idea Speeler, I'll go to the pantry and get it, along with the Mason jar filled with water from the basement, the three battery operated candles, my grandfather's magic wand and the epitome of a fish. You stay here and guard the rest of our ingredients, Speeler."

When Devo returned, he placed all the ingredients for the incantation at the edge of the desk. Devo placed the three candles in a triangle and the Mason jar filled with water in the center of the triangle. He placed the epitome of the Orca on top of the Mason jar and carefully added the jar of pickled pig's feet on top of the picture of the Orca. The other special ingredients were laid around the Mason jar and the jar of pickled pig's feet.

After Devo lit the candles, he looked at Speeler and said, "Everything is ready Speeler, I just need to make my wish known."

"I wish to change the Orca whale I caught in Lowbrook's Pond into a pig."

Devo then waved his grandfather's magic wand and recited the words necessary to cast the spell that he read from the *Book of Magic and Incantations*.

"From the candles, take the fire.

Grant the wish that I desire.

In the center, I have laid.

Orcas to a pig; I want to trade."

Devo repeated the incantation seven times.

"Let's return Mom's pickled pig's feet to the pantry along with everything else we've used and you and I can go down to the pond and see if my incantation worked," Devo said.

"Do you think we could open that jar of pickled pig feet, I certainly would like to taste some," Speeler barked.

"Absolutely not Speeler, I'll give you some dog food if you're that hungry, Devo said.

"I'll pass on the dog food," Speeler barked.

When Speeler and Devo had returned everything to their proper place, then they ran down to Lowbrook's Pond to see if the incantation worked.

Speeler and Devo looked out over the pond to where they could see the Orcas swimming and blowing fountains of water into the air as they swam around the deepest part of the pond.

Devo recited the incantation repeatedly along with Speeler who's barking turned into a howl. Suddenly the Orca whale was covered with an iridescent green light and it disappeared in a puff of smoke in the water.

Speeler and Devo could hear the far-off grunting of a pig. They sat and watched as the really big pig swam to shore, sniffing the ground and grunting.

The Really Big Pig Swam To Shore.

"Good job Devo; we don't have an Orca to worry about now," Speeler barked.

It was just a little after lunch and Devo and Speeler were lying in the shade side by side resting after their ordeal with the Orcas and an afternoon of tossing ball.

"Devo! Devo! Devo, where are you? I need your help. Hurry, there's a really big pig in my vegetable garden eating everything and tramping everything down with his big feet," Devo's mother called out frantically.

"Oh! Oh! That's Mother calling and it sounds like she has a problem," Devo said.

"We don't have any pigs on this farm," Speeler barked.

"Wrong, Speeler, I think we turned one loose this morning at Lowbrook's Pond."

Speeler and Devo ran to the back of the house to where Devo's mother was chasing a big fat pig out of her vegetable garden with a hoe.

The really big pig had eaten all of the tomatoes and had knocked down most of the corn to eat the ears.

The pig was now snorting and rooting out some of the other plants with his nose in the remainder of the garden.

Chapter 16

CORRECTING THINGS GONE WRONG

evo took the hoe from his mother's hands and with Speeler's help; they chased the pig into the barn.

"What now?" Speeler barked.

"Do you know where we might find some cat hair, Speeler?"

"Mr. & Mrs. Watkins have a cat named "Angelina" who sleeps on the front porch swing of their home. Perhaps we can find some of Angelina's hair on the swing covers," Speeler barked.

"What do you want cat hair for?" Speeler barked.

"I think I need to change this pig into a cat."

"Wow, that's a great idea; when Squirrel gets tired, I can chase the cat," Speeler barked.

Speeler and Devo locked the barn and walked down the road to Mr. and Mrs. Watkins home. The Watkins were sitting on the front porch swing and Angelina was sleeping on Mrs. Watkins lap.

"You sit here Speeler and I will go up on the porch and get some hair from Angelina, and be sure to bark for me in about 5 minutes so I can leave." Devo said to his dog, Speeler.

"Good morning Mr. and Mrs. Watkins; Speeler and I were just taking a walk and I thought I would stop and say good morning to you," Devo said.

"That's so very nice of you to stop, Devo; why don't you sit here on the porch swing with us for a while?" Mrs. Watkins said.

"Can I hold Angelina?" Devo said as he sat down on the swing. "Angelina would love that, Mr. Watkins said, she just loves to be held and petted."

Devo sat down on the swing and held Angelina on his lap and as he patted her, he was careful to brush some of her hair onto his clothing.

The Watkins asked about Devo's mother and father and about his grandfather. Devo had just told them about the pig in his mother's vegetable garden when Speeler started barking.

"I had better go Mr. and Mrs. Watkins, Speeler would like to get back home as I think he is getting tired and thirsty," Devo said.

Devo and Speeler went directly to the barn to check on the pig when they left the Watkins's home.

"You stay here in the barn, Speeler, while I go to the house and get all of the articles that we will need for our incantation," Devo said.

Devo ran to the house, went directly to his bedroom, and retrieved the epitome of the Orca and his backpack. He went to his grandfather's study and placed the magic wand in his backpack.

Devo went to the basement, took a Mason jar, filled it with water and placed it in his backpack.

In the dining room, Devo picked up the three batteries operated candles and placed them in his backpack along with the pickled pig's feet from the pantry.

Devo returned to the barn and arranged the three candles on the three points of the triangle, he then added the white paper circle and the Mason jar filled with water and placed them in the center of the circle. He placed the epitome of the Orca on top of the Mason jar and carefully added the jar of pickled pig's feet on top of the picture of the Orca.

Devo removed one of Angelina's cat hairs from his pants and placed it on top of the jar of pickled pig's feet. The other special ingredients were laid around the Mason jar and the jar of pickled pig's feet.

After Devo lit the battery-operated candles, he looked at Speeler and said, "Everything is ready Speeler, I just need to make my wish known and repeat the words I have copied from the. *Book of Magic and Incantations.*

"I will repeat the words I have written down for our incantation seven times and then we should have a cat.

"I wish to change this pig into a long tail cat," Devo said.

"Why are you making a long-tailed cat?" Speeler barked.

"There are a lot of cats in our neighborhood and I want to be sure we can identify this one, easily," Devo said.

Devo then waved his grandfather's magic wand and recited the words necessary to cast the spell that he had copied from the *Book of Magic and Incantations.*

From the candles, take the fire.

Grant the wish that I desire.

In the center, I have laid.

Pig to cat; I want to trade.

Devo repeated the incantation seven times.

Suddenly the pig was covered with an iridescent green light.

The pig disappeared in a puff of smoke; magically, Speeler and Devo could suddenly see a long tail cat appear from the smoke.

A Long Tail Cat Appeared From The Smoke.

"Good job Devo; we don't have a pig to worry about now," Speeler barked.

"Let's return Mom's pickled pig's feet to the pantry along with everything else we've used and then you and I can go out in the yard and play ball again," Devo said.

"You don't suppose I can sample the pickled pig's feet, do you?" Speeler asked in a begging manner.

"Absolutely not," Devo said.

The cat looked at Speeler and Devo, hissed several times and then ran out of the barn.

Chapter 17

A TROUBLESOME CAT

Several weeks had passed before Devo had saved enough of his allowance to walk to town and buy some ice cream for Speeler and him. They were discussing what flavors they were going to order when they came upon Mr. and Mrs. Watkins walking down the sidewalk arm and arm.

"Good morning Mr. and Mrs. Watkins; how is Angelina today?" Speeler barked.

"Good morning to you Devo and also to you Speeler," Mrs. Watkins said.

"You're out walking a little early this morning, aren't you?" Devo asked.

"Oh yes Devo, we had to leave our home; there is a cat that sleeps on our porch swing now and meows constantly, Mr. Watkins said.

"Oh, oh, Speeler barked.

"Is the cat the same color as Angelina and has a very long tail?" Devo asked.

"It looks exactly like Angelina; except that it does have an extremely long tail for a house cat, Mrs. Watkins said.

"Do you know who the cat belongs to, Devo?"

"Well not exactly Mrs. Watkins, but I think I will be able to get rid of it for you," Devo said.

"That would be so nice of you Devo. Mr. Watkins and I are not getting any sleep at night due to that cats meowing," Mr. Watkins said.

"I'll tend to it immediately Mr. and Mrs. Watkins," Devo said.

"I definitely think there is something wrong with the spells I am casting, Speeler."

"I think you are right Devo," Speeler barked.

"We will need to catch that cat, Speeler. Do you have any ideas?"

"Well, if you open the barn door and then hide behind it, I shall find the long tail cat and see if I can chase him into the barn. As soon as he's in the barn, you slam the door shut, Devo," Speeler barked.

"You go look for the long tail cat, Speeler, I will go to the house and gather all the things we need to cast the new spell. When I am ready, I will open the barn door. As soon as you see the barn door open you chase the cat into the barn, Devo said.

"Sounds like a plan," Speeler barked.

Speeler found the long tail cat sitting on the porch swing at Mr. and Mrs. Watkins house. The longtail cat was meowing at the top of his voice. When Speeler walked up on the porch, the long tail cat, hissed at Speeler, jumped off the swing and ran into the yard.

Speeler was barking merrily as he chased the long tail cat across the field toward the barn. This is fun Speeler thought; this is more fun than chasing Squirrel.

It took several tries before Speeler was able to get the long tail cat to seek shelter in the barn.

"Close the door, close the door," Speeler barked.

Devo and Speeler stood in the shadows by the door waiting for the long tail cat to calm himself down after the tiring chase by Speeler.

Devo had placed an old winter jacket that hung in the barn in the center of the floor. He then placed a small bowl of milk alongside of the winter jacket.

The long tail cat stood and watched Devo and Speeler for some time before he knew it was safe to drink the milk. When he had finished the milk, the long tail cat was tired from his chase by Speeler and now that his stomach was full; he laid down on the winter jacket and soon fell asleep.

As soon as the long tail cat fell asleep, Devo walked up and very gently picked the long tail cat up in his arms and patted him gently. The long tail cat began to purr and soon fell back to sleep. Devo removed several hairs from the cat and returned the long tail cat back to the winter jacket lying in the center of the barn floor.

"Any suggestion Speeler as to what we should try to change the long tail cat into?" Devo asked.

Speeler looked around the barn to see if anything stored there might give him inspiration as to what they should do. Lying on the floor in the dust by an empty bushel basket, Speeler's eyes fell upon a white feather.

"How about a chicken? I see a white feather over there so we won't even have to leave the barn to find something," Speeler barked.

"Great idea Speeler; I feel certain that a chicken will give us no trouble." Devo said.

Devo walked over, picked up the white feather and placed it with the items he had brought from the house.

Devo arranged the three candles on the three points of the triangle, he then added the white paper circle and the Mason jar filled with water and placed them in the center of the circle. He placed the epitome of the Orca on top of the Mason jar and carefully added the jar of pickled pig's feet on top of that.

Devo placed one of Angelina's cat hairs on top of the jar of pickled pig's feet. Devo then took the hair that he had taken from long tail cat and placed it across the top of Angelina's cat hair.

As a final ingredient Devo, carefully placed the white feather from the barn floor on top of the long tail cat's hair. The other special ingredients were laid around the Mason jar and the jar of pickled pig's feet.

After Devo lit the battery-operated candles, he looked at Speeler and said, "Everything is ready Speeler. I just need to make my wish known and repeat the words I have copied from the *Book of Magic and Incantations* and say the words I have written down for our incantation.

Chapter 18

THE WISH

"I wish to change this long-tailed cat into a bird like the one from this white feather," Devo said.

"Why are you wishing for a bird like the one from this white feather?" Speeler barked.

"There are a lot of chickens in our neighborhood and some of them are very mean. This white feather came from our farm and I know our chickens are all very gentle," Devo said.

Devo then waved his grandfather's magic wand and recited the words necessary to cast the spell that he had copied from the *Book of Magic and Incantations*.

"From the candles, take the fire.

Grant the wish that I desire.

In the center, I have laid.

Long tail cat to bird like my white feather; I want to trade."

Devo repeated the incantation seven times.

Suddenly the long tail cat was covered with an iridescent green light and disappeared in a puff of smoke.

Speeler and Devo could see a large white bird standing on the winter jacket where the long tail cat had been.

The thing that Devo had created stood up, shook and extended his long necked. As the cloud of smoke arose to the top of the barn both

Devo and Speeler were stunned to see a goose standing in place of the long tail cat.

Devo And Speeler Were Both Stunned To See A Goose

The goose looked at Speeler and Devo, honked, hissed several times, flapped his wings and flew out the open barn window.

"Oh, oh, that didn't go well at all," Speeler barked.

"I did not remember until just now that two years ago we had a mean old white goose named Jason that Mother fixed for Thanksgiving dinner. I had forgotten all about him. Unfortunately, Speeler, that must have been one of Jason's down feathers that we picked up for our incantation," Devo said sorrowfully.

Therefore, I think we should name this goose "Jasontwo."

"What will we do now?" Speeler barked.

"Let's you and I go sit on the front porch and talk this over before we do anything," Devo said.

zzzDevo and Speeler sat on the front porch and talked over the new glitch in their attempt to correct the events resulting from their fishing adventure.

Devo's grandfather opened the screen door, walked out onto the porch and sat down beside Speeler and Devo.

"What are you two up to today?" Grandfather asked.

Oh, Grandfather I have gotten myself into a lot of trouble and I need someone to talk to," Devo said.

"That's what Grandfathers are for Devo; tell me what your problem is and I will see if I can help."

"Well, Grandfather, it all started several weeks ago when Speeler and I wanted to go fishing; do you remember that day?" Devo asked.

"Yes, I remember it very well. It was the day I drove to town to do some errands."

Devo put his arms around his grandfather and begin to tell him the story about performing the magic to be sure there were fish in Lowbrook's Pond.

Devo told his grandfather how he performed the magic and about the Orca, the pig, the long tail cat and now the big white goose.

"You see Grandfather; I thought for sure the white feather was from one of our white Leghorn Chickens but much to my surprise it must have been from that mean old goose, Jason. I am calling this goose Jasontwo," Devo said.

"I see no problem with having a goose in the farmyard, Grandfather said. We shall feed it, shelter it and treat it exactly as any good farmer would do," Grandfather said.

"What concerns me about your whole episode of magic and incantations is if you expect to become a sorcerer like your grandfather, you will need to spend more time planning and following the details as set down in the *Book of Magic and Incantations*. I think it's much like your teacher told you about your math test, Devo; the end result is much the same but what you did in the middle did not follow the rules," Grandfather said.

"First of all, you must consider the effects of your actions upon other people; which you did not do. Secondly, you must learn to follow instructions."

"I thought we did a good job of following the instructions," Speeler barked.

"What is Speeler barking about?" Grandfather asked.

"Speeler is of the opinion that we did follow the instructions as best we could," Devo replied.

"I hardly think a jar of pickled pigs' feet qualifies as the hair of the pig," Grandfather said.

"I shall need to give you and Speeler a lesson in considering the effects of your actions upon other people and following instructions," Grandfather said.

Chapter 19

THE LESSON

"How would you give us a lesson, grandfather?" Devo asked.

"I shall have you bake a cake," Grandfather said.

"Bake a cake?" Can I have some when it's finished?" Speeler barked in a soft tone as he murmured to Devo, so that Grandfather would not hear him.

"What is Speeler babbling about," Grandfather asked.

"Speeler wants to know how you are going to teach me a lesson by baking a cake," Devo said.

"Devo and Speeler, I want you to come into the house and we shall get started on our baking project."

Grandfather walked to the pantry and opened a little tin box that sat on the top shelf. He opened the container, withdrew a recipe card and handed it to Devo.

"I would like you and Speeler to bake this cake," Grandfather said.

Devo took the cake recipe from Grandfather and read it.

"I am not really a baker, Grandfather; however, I think Speeler and I can do this," Devo said.

"We are both going to make a chocolate cake," Grandfather said.

Grandfather handed Devo the recipe for the chocolate cake. Then he asked Devo to assemble all of the ingredients that he would need to bake the cake and place them on the kitchen table.

"When you have all the ingredients on the kitchen table call me; I will be on the porch watching Jasontwo, our new goose."

Devo went into the kitchen, opened the pantry door and started his search for the ingredients to make the chocolate cake.

The recipe called for 6 ounces of semi-sweet chocolate. The only thing that Devo could find was a plastic container of Hershey chocolate topping which he placed on the table.

The recipe called for 2/3 cup of shortening. Devo's mother did not have enough shortening in the can to make two thirds of a cup so Devo made up the shortage with lard.

Devo measured out the flour, sugar and salt and placed it on the kitchen table. Devo did not have the soda that the recipe called for so he used 1 teaspoon of Pepsi, as he knew it was called, "Soda Pop."

Everyone had cereal with milk for breakfast that morning and there was no milk left in the refrigerator; therefore, Devo substituted water.

The recipe called for three eggs; there were only two eggs left in the refrigerator so Devo took the two eggs and measured out powdered eggs for the third egg.

Devo found the red food coloring and the vanilla extract, which he placed on the table.

There was no whipping cream in the refrigerator so Devo placed a pint container of cream on the kitchen table along with the other ingredients; thinking he would whip it later.

Devo walked out onto the front porch and called his grandfather. "Grandfather I have everything on the kitchen table so I am ready to bake my cake."

I will be right there, Devo, I want to see how you make your cake," Grandfather said.

When Devo's grandfather entered the room, Devo asked him if he could borrow his magic wand.

"Are you going to use the magic wand to make your cake, Devo?" Grandfather asked.

"Oh yes, Grandfather; I can make a fine cake with the ingredients and the magic wand," Devo said.

Devo placed the recipe on top of the table and stacked all the ingredients on top of the recipe.

Devo arranged the three battery operated candles in a triangular shape, as Devo had done in his previous incantations. He placed the recipe on top of the table and stacked all the ingredients on top of the recipe.

Devo knew that he did not have all the correct ingredients and had been forced to make a few substitutions; however, in the end, he knew the magic wand would take care of the problem.

Devo lit the battery-operated candles, looked at Grandfather and said, "Everything is ready, I just need to make my wish known and repeat the words I have copied from your *Book of Magic and Incantations.*

"I wish to change the ingredients on top of this recipe into a chocolate cake," Devo said.

"Is this going to be like your wishing for a chicken from the white feather we found on the barn floor?" Speeler barked.

Devo ignored Speeler and began to wave his grandfather's magic wand and recited the words necessary to cast the spell that he had copied from the *Book of Magic and Incantations.*

"From the candles, take the fire.

Grant the wish that I desire.

In the center, there to make.

Ingredients that I want to make into a cake."

Devo repeated the incantation seven times.

Suddenly the ingredients were covered with a green iridescent light and disappeared in a puff of smoke.

Chapter 20

THE TASTE TEST

Grandfather and Devo could see a four-layer chocolate cake setting on the table in the place of the ingredients that Devo had assembled.

Devo explained to his grandfather that the recipe had instructions to cover the cake and put it in the refrigerator for eight hours before serving. The cake was placed in the refrigerator after which Devo and his grandfather cleaned up the kitchen.

"I'm all finished now, Grandfather, what were you going to teach me?" Devo asked.

"That you shall learn tomorrow Devo; as for now, you and I are going to town and do a little shopping," Grandfather said.

At the grocery store, Grandfather purchased:

One small can of shortening.
One bag of flour.
One bag of sugar.
A box of salt.
One can of baking soda.
1/2 gallon of milk.
One dozen medium-sized eggs.
One tube of red food coloring.
One package of unsweetened chocolate.

One package of cream cheese.
One box of brown sugar.
One container of whipping cream.
Two bars of semi-sweet chocolate.
One box of baking soda.

When they arrived home, Devo and his grandfather put all of the groceries on the kitchen table and Grandfather began to make the batter for his cake.

Devo's grandfather followed the directions very carefully and when he took his cake out of the oven, he put it in the refrigerator alongside of Devo's chocolate cake.

"You are all finished Grandfather so what is it you were you going to teach me?" Devo asked.

"That you shall learn tomorrow Devo; as for now, you and I are going out on the front porch and look at the clouds to see what magical shapes we can find."

The next morning Devo was up at the crack of dawn and he was sitting on the front porch waiting for his grandfather to wake up and join him.

"Grandfather, what am I going to learn today?" Devo asked.

"What I have to teach you, you shall learn after dinner this evening," Grandfather said.

"You and Speeler can spend the day playing and we shall talk after dinner this evening when we are joined by your mother and father."

Devo ate his dinner very fast and when he was finished, he repeatedly asked his mother, his father and his grandfather, "Are you finished yet?" Devo was anxious to hear what his grandfather had to tell him.

Finally, everyone finished dinner and Grandfather said, "This evening we shall have desserts prepared by Devo and me."

Grandfather left the table went to the kitchen refrigerator and set the two chocolate cakes on the counter.

Grandfather withdrew eight china plates from the cupboard and placed them on the counter.

Grandfather placed a "D" on the bottom of the four plates with a red crayon and placed a slice of Devo's cake on each plate.

Grandfather then placed a "G" on the bottom of the four remaining plates with a red crayon and placed a slice of his cake on each plate.

The Chocolate Cakes

Making two trips, Grandfather carried all eight plates into the dining room.

"I would like everyone at the table to taste the cake on each of the plates and then tell me which of them taste the best.

Everyone at the table sat quietly as they tested their two samples of chocolate cake.

"I really like this one Devo's mother said, as she took another bite. "The other one tasted kind of flat and I didn't really like it."

"Well I like this one, Devo's father said, I really didn't care for the other one."

"This one was the best," Devo said as he held up his plate. Grandfather tasted both slices of chocolate cake, "I really like this one," as he placed the last bite into his mouth.

"What's this all about?" Devo's mother inquired.

"This is a lesson in magic; I am training Devo to be my apprentice and this is one of the lessons that he must learn," Grandfather said.

"I'm going to need to know how to make chocolate cakes, Grandfather?"

"No, my son, the lesson you must learn is written on the bottom of each dish. If you will turn over the dish that held your favorite chocolate cake; tell me what you see on the bottom of the plate," Grandfather said.

"Why there is a "G" written with a red crayon on the bottom of my plate," Devo's mother said.

"There is also a "G" on the bottom of my plate Devo's," father said. "There is a "G" on my plate too, Grandfather," Devo said.

"The chocolate cake that I liked the best was also on a plate that had a "G" written on it.

"What does the "G" stand for?" Devo's mother asked.

"The "G" stands for Grandfather," Grandfather said.

"But I don't understand Grandfather what is there to learn from eating the chocolate cake?" Devo asked.

"Everyone here has agreed that the chocolate cake that I've made was the best."

"I planned ahead, went to the grocery store and purchased all the ingredients I would need for the recipe."

"I followed the recipe by doing exactly what it called for," Grandfather said.

"I made no substitutions, performed no incantations nor used any magic."

"My magic, if any, came from preparing for the task at hand, assembling the correct ingredients and following the instructions," Grandfather said.

"You on the other hand Devo, tried to paint the barn red with a can of blue paint and attempt to make it work using magic. Magic does not work that way."

"Real magic in life, Devo, comes from preparing yourself for an opportunity. When the opportunity comes you need to take the necessary steps to reach your goal successfully."

"I shall try to remember that Grandfather; though, it seems so easy for me to take a shortcut," Devo said regretfully.

Chapter 21

A LESSON LEARNED

After the dinner dishes were cleared from the table, Devo and Speeler went out and sat on the front porch to watch the sunset on the White Rock Mountains.

They had been sitting there for some time thinking about the events of the evening when Devo turned to Speeler and said, "Did you learn anything this evening, Speeler?" Devo asked.

"Yes, as a matter of fact I did," Speeler barked.

"What did you learn Speeler?"

"I learned that you are a lousy cook and an even worse magician," Speeler barked with a doggie grin on his face.

"Did you learn anything, Devo?" Speeler barked.

"As a matter of fact, I did Speeler."

"What did you learn?"

"I learned that I never want to be a cook or a chemist," Devo said.

"Why do you say that?" Speeler barked.

"Because Speeler, I don't think in precise measurements."

"How do you think?" Speeler asked.

"To me 100+150 does not add up to 250. To me it would add to something between 225 and 275, if you catch my meaning."

"In that case I don't think you should become an accountant either unless you plan to work for organized crime," Speeler barked as he smiled at Devo.

Just then, Jasontwo entered the yard with his wings outspread, honking, squawking, hissing and flapping his wings like a helicopter about to take off.

"What's his problem?" Speeler barked.

"Gosh! I don't have any idea, Speeler," Devo said.

Jasontwo came to the foot of the front porch steps with his wings outspread, honking, squawking, hissing and flapping his wings.

Devo got up on the steps and started to walk towards Jasontwo.

Jasontwo bit down on Devo's pants leg shook his head and continued squawking and flapping his wings. It was only after Speeler came down from the porch, stood between Jasontwo and Devo and growled furiously that Jasontwo retreated to the backyard.

"What was that all about?" Devo asked.

"I don't have the foggiest idea," Speeler remarked. "I will walk to the backyard and see what's going on.

Speeler was gone about 10 minutes, before he returned and sat down on the porch next to Devo. Speeler sat there for a while without saying anything.

"Well! What did you find out Mr. Speeler?" Devo asked.

"You will never guess what that crazy goose has done," Speeler barked.

"Is there any chance you're going to tell me?" Devo said sarcastically.

"It appears that I have been evicted from my dog house. He has taken the place over and will not let me go near it. To top it off he is drinking my water and he ate all of my dog food," Speeler barked.

"I'll go in the house and talk to Dad about it; maybe he can do something or have a suggestion as to what we can do with Jasontwo," Devo said as he opened the screen door and walked into the house.

Devo's father was sitting reading the evening paper in the living room when Devo found him.

"Dad, do you have a minute?" Devo asked.

"Surely Son, what do you need, Devo's father said as he lay down his newspaper.

"Dad, it seems that Jasontwo has taken over Speeler's dog house, is eating his dog food and will not let anyone go near him. Now Speeler will not have a place to sleep or eat," Devo said.

"I will go out and see what I can do."

Devo's father headed off for the backyard while Devo and Speeler sat on the steps of the front porch. They could hear a lot of hissing, squawking, honking and occasionally the voice of Devo's father yelling at Jasontwo.

When Devo's father returned to the front porch he sat down next to Devo and said, "I'm sorry Son but Jasontwo is not going to give up Speeler's dog house without me inflicting some physical harm to him. I suggest that temporarily we put Speeler in the barn and find him a water bowl and a food dish," Devo's father said sorrowfully.

"I can take care of that Dad. I will get Speeler something to eat and drink out of and I can leave the barn door partially open so he can get in and out," Devo said.

"Why do I have to give up my dog house, why can't that crazy goose sleep in the barn?" Speeler barked angrily.

"I will tell you like it is Speeler, if you have decided that you cannot live without your dog house and your water and food dish, I suggest that you go in the backyard and chase that Mr. Jasontwo into the barn, Devo said as he leaned over and whispered in Speeler's ear.

Speeler sat for a while thinking and then he barked "I think the barn will temporarily be just fine."

Chapter 22

EVICTED

The next morning, Devo went out to the barn and filled Speeler's water dish with some fresh water and put some food in his doggie dish. Devo then got a coffee can of chicken feed and went to feed Jasontwo who was lying on the rug in Speeler's dog house.

When Devo reached over to pour the chicken feed in the dish for Jasontwo, Jasontwo jumped from the dog house flapped his wings squealed, hissed and honked loudly. He ran over and bit down on Devo's finger.

"OUCH, you dumb bird! You bit my finger; that's the last time I'll try to feed you," Devo said as he walked away looking at his finger to see if it was bleeding.

Devo went to the house where his mother put some antibiotic salve on the wound and wrapped it with a Band-Aid.

"Thank you, Mother, for fixing my finger; that's the last time I'll feed that goose in Speeler's bowl. Next time I'll spill it in the grass and he can come and get it when I leave."

"By the way Mother, are we doing anything special for Father's birthday this year?" Devo asked.

"Yes, I am planning to throw a surprise party for your father and I have invited your uncle and aunt to come and have their evening meal with us," Devo's mother said.

"Have you planned your evening meal yet, Mother?"

"Yes, I have everything planned except for the meat."

"How about goose Mother?" Devo asked hopefully thinking that Jasontwo might serve as the main course.

"I think that would be a great idea, Devo but, your father does not like goose. Since it is his birthday, I think I should serve something that he likes," Devo's mother said.

"Have you narrowed it down to any particular meat, Mother?"

"Well the possibilities are steak, fish, chicken, lamb and possibly Turkey," Devo's mother said.

"Maybe I can help you out Mother without Dad knowing that you are planning a surprise party for him." Devo said.

"How would you plan to do that?" Devo's mother asked.

"I would tell him that me and some of my friends are working on a project concerning the eating habits of Americans. I would then simply ask him what his favorite meat is." Devo said.

It was several weeks before Devo found his father alone reading the newspaper.

"Dad, do you think you could help me with a little assignment that I have?" Devo asked.

"Certainly Son, how can I help you?"

"We are gathering information on people's likes and dislikes, so I will ask you a few questions on what you like most and what you dislike the most," Devo said.

"The first question is what is your favorite color?"

"I would say my favorite color is blue."

"Next, what is your favorite flavor of ice cream?"

"Peach is my favorite."

"What is your favorite meat for dinner?"

"I will have to think on this one a little bit; I think it will have to be your mother's meatloaf."

"What is your favorite vegetable?"

"That's easy; it's corn on the cob."

"That's all the questions I have Dad, thank you so much for your help," Devo said.

Devo and Speeler walked out to the front porch and Devo sat down on the steps.

"Boy, that was disappointing. I was hoping that Dad's favorite meat would be goose."

"Well, it was a long shot to say the least, now what?" Speeler barked.

"What are we going to do with that goose?"

"He is eating us out of house and home, he bit my finger and he has made you live in the barn." Devo said.

"Think you could turn him into a platter of meatloaf?" Speeler barked.

"I don't think that's going to be possible. I think at this point the only thing I'm going to be able to do is to change his form," Devo said.

"We need to get rid of him, that's for sure. Let me think," Speeler barked.

Speeler sat on the front porch steps with his two paws out in front of him and laid his head on his paws. It was very quiet and Speeler laid there for some time. Speeler finally raised his head up and looked at Devo. "I've got a great idea, let's give him away," Speeler barked.

"I think that's a great idea, Speeler. Let's get your doggie travel cage out of the barn. If I opened the cage door and placed it in front of the dog house when he comes out in the morning Jasontwo will walk into the doggie travel cage and I can catch him."

"After you capture him in the doggie travel cage how do you plan to get rid of him?" Speeler barked.

"You and I are going to make a sign that says goose for sale $3. Then We hike down to State Route 18 and sell him to some passing motorists for their Thanksgiving dinner," Devo said.

"How did you decide on a price of three dollars?" Speeler barked. "Very simple my good friend; as that is the exact price of two Eskimo Pies from the ice cream man," Devo said as he licked his lips.

Devo and Speeler went to the barn and placed the doggie travel cage in the middle of the floor. Devo took a sheet of wrapping paper and cut it to the size of the side of the doggie travel cage. Devo wrote in big black letters:

For Sale
Thanksgiving Goose
$3.00

"You think somebody's dumb enough to pay three dollars for that goose?" Speeler barked.

"Well some circus guy once said, "There is a sucker born every minute," Devo replied.

"What's a sucker?" Speeler asked.

"You are going to find the answer to that Speeler just as soon as we sell Jasontwo."

That evening as it grew dark and Jasontwo had settled in the dog house for the evening, Devo took the dog traveling cage out to the backyard, and placed it against the front opening of Speeler's dog house.

Chapter 23

GOOSE FOR SALE

Devo was up bright and early Saturday morning, he ran to the barn, got Speeler and headed to Speeler's dog house to see if Jasontwo was in the dog traveling cage.

"It doesn't look like he's in the cage, Devo. Let me get behind the dog house and you get as close to this dog traveling cage as you can and start barking. I think he will come out and try to run you away," Devo said.

When everything was ready, Speeler started barking as loud as he could, "You can't catch me, you can't catch me, you can't catch me."

Jasontwo came out of the dog house squealing, yelling, honking, flapping his wings and hissing.

As soon as Jasontwo was in the dog traveling cage, Devo came from behind the dog house and shut the door on the cage.

"I have you now, you nasty old goose," Devo said smiling.

"Good job," Speeler barked.

"I'll go tell Mom that we are walking to town to get rid of Jasontwo and then you and I will see if we can sell him," Devo said.

Devo told his mother that Speeler and he were going to take Jasontwo in his wagon to town and try to sell him. Devo loaded the dog travel cage, some string and an empty feed sack into his wagon. Speeler and Devo walked down the lane headed for State Route 18.

It took nearly a half hour for Speeler and Devo to reach the corner of North Street and State Route 18. Devo had chosen this spot because this was a four-way stop. It wasn't long before the first car stopped and the man got out and approached Devo.

"Is that your goose?" The man asked.

"Yes Sir, it is," Devo responded.

"Why are you selling him?" The man asked.

"I am really not able to take care of him any longer and I want to see that he gets a good home," Devo said.

"You're only asking three dollars for him?" The man asked.

"Yes sir, for three dollars he will be yours," Devo said hopefully.

The man reached for his wallet and pulled out three crisp one-dollar bills and handed them to Devo.

"If you will hold the sack for me, I will reach in the cage and put him in the sack," the man said.

The man reached in the cage, grabbed Jasontwo by the feet and put him in the sack so quickly that Jasontwo had hardly time to hiss or flap his wings.

The man tied the top of the feed sack with the piece of string and placed it in his trunk.

"Are you sure that's all you want for this goose. I really believe it's worth more than that," the man said sympathetically.

"No Sir, three dollars is all I want and I want to thank you for buying him," Devo said. The man got in his car and drove away.

"Jump in the wagon Speeler let's go find the ice cream man."

Speeler barked smiling. "I understand now what that man from the circus meant."

Things were going great for Speeler and Devo.

School had started and the leaves were turning color and slowly falling from the branches of the trees.

Jasontwo was gone, Speeler was out of the barn and he was back in his dog house again.

Devo was glad to be back with his friends after school started. Devo walked home from school on Friday with Kevin and Julie Meyer.

Devo was very fond of Kevin mostly because he always talked about interesting things; it was his younger sister that got on Devo's nerves.

She was always trying to hang around him and be his friend and several times she had asked herself over to Devo house or to her house to play with her in their treehouse. What would the guys at school think if they saw me playing with a girl? Devo thought.

"You want to come over to my house after school and play in the treehouse, Devo?" Julie asked.

"No Julie, I have things I need to do," Devo said.

"Can I come over and help you?"

"No Julie," Devo replied sarcastically.

"I just thought I'd ask, Devo," Julie said apologetically.

"Is that all you have on your mind Julie; don't you ever talk about anything else?

"I talk about a lot of things Devo."

"Like what?"

"Well, for instance, do you know how to get down off of an elephant?" Julie said smiling.

"I have never been on an elephant, Julie."

"Neither have I, Devo, but I know how to do it."

"All right Miss smarty how do you get down off of an elephant?" Devo said skeptically.

"The thing is Devo; you do not get down off of an elephant; you get down off of a goose." Julie said as she turned and walked up the sidewalk to her house.

"See you tomorrow, Devo, Julie yelled as she entered the house. "How was school today, honey?" Devo's mother asked as he sat drinking his milk.

"I had a great day today Mom; I hit a home run at lunch and the bases were loaded. Our team won 6 to 4."

"Why did you walk home instead of riding the bus?" Devo's mother asked.

"I walked home with Kevin and Julie Meyer. Kevin was telling me about a mastodon that they were digging up in the ice in Siberia."

"Did Julie walk home with you?" Devo's mother asked.

"Yes, Mother, she did; she's a real dork; do you know what she asked me?" Devo said as he ate his last cookie.

"I surely don't Devo; what did she ask you?"

"She wanted to know if I knew how to get down off of an elephant."

"Did you know the answer?" Devo's mother asked smiling.

"No Mother, I have never been on an elephant."

"You don't get down off of an elephant Devo, you get down off of a goose," Devo's mother said as she put her arms around him; giving him a hug.

"That's the same thing Julie told me. I don't get it Mom," Devo said in a disgusted voice.

"It's a play on words, Devo; there is the down as in, "I fell down" and there is the "Down" as in goose feathers that they stuff pillows with."

Devo sat for a long time repeating the question that Julie had asked him.

"Maybe Julie is a little smarter than I give her credit for; if she weren't a girl, I might play with her," Devo said to his mother.

Chapter 24

IN THE DOG HOUSE AGAIN

It was just a few days after Halloween when Devo's grandfather knocked at his bedroom door early one Saturday morning. "Devo are you awake?"

"Yes Grandfather, I am up and dressed and I will be down just as soon as I make my bed," Devo said.

"I think you had better leave your bed go for a while; Speeler has been barking at something and I think you should go down and see what his problem is," Grandfather said.

Devo went downstairs out the front door and into the back yard. Speeler was seated about 10 feet in front of his dog house barking furiously.

"What's the problem, Speeler?" Devo called.

"That confounded goose is back and he has run me out of my home again," Speeler barked.

"I will go to the barn and get the dog traveling cage and we will catch him again, Devo called back to Speeler as he turned to run to the barn.

Devo opened the door of the doggie traveling cage and placed it in front of the dog house, exactly as they had done before. Speeler started barking to lured Jasontwo into the cage.

"This time I will ask 6 dollars. I will need three dollars to return to the first man that bought him. I will need to return that money if we can find him. The additional 3 dollars is for two Eskimo Pies." Devo said.

"I like your thinking," Speeler barked.

Speeler and Devo put Jasontwo in a feed sack, placed him in the wagon and headed for State Route 18 and North Street.

As they passed the service station on their way to State Route 18, they overheard the attendant and the driver of the delivery truck talking.

"I'm going to Nashville, Tennessee for my next stop. I will see you in about two weeks so if you need anything be sure to call and order it; then I will bring it on my next stop," the truck driver said.

"Do you think Jasontwo will be feeling "Down" if we send him to Nashville?" Speeler barked.

"I suspect Jasontwo will be a little "Down" in the mouth for a while, Devo said laughing out loud."

Devo waited until the driver was just about ready to pull away from the curb when he grabbed the feed sack containing Jasontwo, and tossed it in the back of the truck.

"Come on Speeler I'll treat you to an Eskimo pie."

It was two weeks before Thanksgiving, and Devo's father invited him to go along on a hunting trip to Van Wert County. Mr. Mannix and two of his law partners were planning to hunt pheasant. Devo would not be allowed to carry a gun or shoot but his father thought that it would be a good learning experience for him.

Devo had fashioned a rifle out of some scrap lumber he had taken from the old chicken coop.

Every day after school Devo and Speeler would play in the hayloft in the barn. Speeler would pretend that he was the turkey and Devo would attempt to get him in the sight of his make-believe gun.

From out in the yard Devo and Speeler both heard a familiar sound. They looked at each other and Devo shook his head saying no, no, no; it can't be.

Honk, honk, honk! Honk, honk, honk! Honk, honk, honk!

"Did you hear that," Speeler barked.

"I'm sorry to say Speeler that I did. I cannot believe that goose has walked back here from Nashville, Tennessee.

"It can't be," Speeler remark.

"I'm afraid it probably is, and I'm thinking you will be sleeping in the barn tonight."

Speeler and Devo walked down into the back yard only to find Jasontwo perched on top of Speeler's dog house.

Chapter 25

THIRD TRY

"What's our next move, Mr. Magician?" Speeler asked.

"Well, I never thought this would happen but as they say "Third time is a charm.""

"Let's go to the house, and I will get on the phone and see if I can research shipping him someplace far away."

Speeler and Devo went to the house and while Devo called shipping companies on the telephone, Speeler laid on the front porch and fell asleep.

Devo researched all the possible methods of transporting Jasontwo to some distant place. He looked at UPS, air transportation, the railroad, US Mail, FedEx and several private corporations that carried animals.

Devo went back on the front porch and woke up Speeler.

"Let's go Speeler I figured out what we're going to do with Jasontwo."

"How are you going to get rid of him?" Speeler asked.

"I have decided to use the railroad; it is by far going to be the cheapest way that I can send Jasontwo to some distant place."

"Let's go to the barn, get the dog traveling cage, the wagon and a feed sack, and we will try to catch Jasontwo once again," Devo said.

It only took about 10 minutes for Devo and Speeler to capture Jasontwo and put him in the sack. Devo put the feed sack containing Jasontwo into the wagon, and they were off to the railroad.

"Why are we stopping here? There is no railway station to purchase a ticket for Jasontwos shipping," Speeler barked.

"Speeler! You know I don't have any money to buy Jasontwo a ticket on the railroad, I spent my last three dollars buying us Eskimo Pies," Devo said.

"Well, how are you going to ship him then?" Speeler asked.

There was a loud clang of the couplings on the railroad cars as the locomotive started slowly to move down the track. Devo lifted the feed sack containing Jasontwo and held it in his hands. As the train slowly picked up speed, Devo walked closer to the boxcars as they moved by.

About 10 boxcars had passed before Devo spotted a boxcar with open doors. Devo turned and ran in the direction of the engine, and when the open boxcar was alongside him; he threw the feed sack containing Jasontwo into the open car.

The train started to pick up speed and it was soon out of sight. "Goodbye Jasontwo, have a nice trip," Devo said as he stood waving goodbye.

"Follow me Speeler, I have just one more thing to find out," Devo said.

"Where are we going?" Speeler asked.

"We are going to the train station to ask Mr. Hank Newman, the station master where that train's next stop will be.

"Good morning Mr. Newman, Devo said as he walked into the train station and approached the ticket window.

"Good morning Devo and good morning to you Speeler; what are you two up to today?" Mr. Newman asked.

"We had a little unfinished business that we needed to take care of further down the track and I was wondering if you could tell where the next stop of the train that just left the station will be." Devo asked.

"That train's next scheduled stop will be in Baltimore, Maryland. Is there any particular reason why you ask Devo?" Hank asked.

"Not really, Mr. Newman, I am just always curious where trains, buses and airplanes are going and where the cargo on them is going."

"Well you and Speeler have a fun day today, Devo," Mr. Newman said.

As Devo and Speeler left the train station, Speeler looked up at Devo and said," Is Baltimore, Maryland a long way from here?"

"Yes Speeler, it's a long… long… long… way from here."

Things got back to normal at the Mannix homestead. Devo and Speeler could now play in the backyard and Speeler had regained possession of his dog house.

It was Sunday morning and Devo was just getting in his car with his family when Speeler ran up and barked at him anxiously.

"Our friend is back; he woke me up this morning and chased me out of bed," Speeler barked sorrowfully.

"I'm sorry Speeler, I am on my way to church I'll take care of it when I get home," Devo said in a disgusted voice.

Devo jumped in the backseat and sat next to Grandfather Mannix. "What was that all about, Devo?" Grandfather asked.

"Jasontwo is back from Baltimore, Maryland," Devo said.

Grandfather did not say anything he just sat, smiled and shook his head.

"Is that dreadful goose back again," Devo's mother asked.

"Yes Mother, I believe he is," Devo said in a half whisper.

"We really need to do something about that goose, he won't even let me hang the laundry out on the clothes line. I like to hang out my sheets and pillowcases when I washed them. I have had to do them in the dryer since that goose has taken over the backyard," Devo's mother said.

"I will take care of it after church today Mother," Devo said.

Devo remained very quiet in the car as his father drove down Shady Lane headed for the church. As they pulled into the parking lot, Devo thought; I think its time for me to talk to Grandfather about Jasontwo. I wish I had done that a long time ago.

Grandfather reached down and took Devo's hand and held it firmly in his.

"I sense that you have a problem Devo, we can talk about it when we get home after church services if you like."

"Thank you, Grandfather," Devo said as he entered the church.

Chapter 26

SEPARATING THE PARTS

When Speeler and Devo walked up on the front porch, Grandfather was sitting in the porch swing reading the Sunday newspaper.

"Grandfather, I'm wondering if you could help me with a little problem that I'm having," Devo said.

"Certainly, tell me all about it."

"Without going into great detail Grandfather; I have used a spell to create something and now I can't get rid of what I created; it keeps coming back."

"Animal, vegetable or mineral," Grandfather asked.

"Animal; in fact, it happens to be Jasontwo."

"I was wondering where that cantankerous old goose came from," Grandfather said.

"Why do you want to get rid of him," Grandfather asked.

"He has taken over Speeler's dog house and Mother and I can't use the backyard without him trying to bite us."

"It is one of the hazards of magic, Devo. Sometimes when you create something, it simply will not go away."

"What do you do when that happens, Grandfather?" Devo asked.

"In my many years of experience Devo, I have found that separating what you have created into parts and then disposing of the parts works the best. You will need to separate the parts; that way the entity is unable to restore itself."

"Thank you, Grandfather. I think I will need to spend considerable time thinking about what you have said. This may be a little more complicated than I thought," Devo said.

Devo went to the barn to find Speeler. He found Speeler in the feed room sleeping on an empty feed sack.

"Is that the best thing you can find to lay on Speeler?" Devo asked. "It's the best thing I could find on short notice. What I like to lay on is the old rug in my dog house," Speeler barked.

"How about coming up in the hayloft and sit with me while I try to make a decision on how to get rid of Jasontwo," Devo asked.

"You lead the way I will be right behind you," Speeler barked.

As Devo and Speeler started to climb up on the bales of hay Speeler perked up his ears and said, "I think somebody just came into the barn."

"Devo are you here in the barn?" Came a voice that Devo did not immediately recognize.

"Who's there?" Devo asked in a very loud voice.

"It's me! Julie Meyer."

Devo looked down at Speeler and said, "That's all I need is that Meyers girl hanging around while I've got a lot on my mind," Devo said in a skeptical voice.

"Give her a chance Devo, you never can tell she may be a lot of help," Speeler barked.

"She's a girl, Speeler, what could she possibly know.

"I think she's pretty smart; you just need to give her a chance," Speeler barked.

"You just like her because she scratches behind your ear," Devo said as he climbed up higher on the bales of hay.

"Where are you, Devo?" Julie called at the top of her voice.

"We are up here sitting on a bale of hay Julie," Devo said.

Devo and Speeler sat down on a bale of hay and in a few minutes, they were joined by Julie Meyer.

Julie sat down next to Speeler and began to scratch his head behind his ears.

"What are you guys up to today?" Julie asked.

"I got a problem I'm working on Julie so don't need a girl to bother me," Devo said in an impolite manner.

"You never know Devo someday you may need a girl to help you and it is possible that you might get to like girls," Julie said in a very soft voice.

"That will be the day," Devo said.

"I think you should be nice to Julie, Devo. She might be very helpful," Speeler barked.

"What is Speeler barking about?" Julie asked.

"He thinks you should go home and play with your dolls."

"I doubt that, Speeler and I get along really well," Julie remarked.

"So, what is the problem you are working on Devo," Julie inquired.

Well Miss Nosy, if you must know, I have a goose named Jasontwo and he has taken over the whole backyard and Speeler's dog house. He is very mean and nasty and will not even let my mother hang her clean sheets out on the clothesline to dry. I need a way to get rid of him."

"Did you ever see one of those horror movies where they cut somebody up and bury all the parts in different places so that the monster can never get himself together again?"

"Yes, I have; so, your problem is, if I understand you correctly, is that you need to get rid of this goose and have his parts separated so they can never get together again; is that correct?"

"That's pretty amazing Julie you seem to catch on quickly. Now, do you have an answer and how I can do that?"

"Well! You could have him for Thanksgiving dinner, throw his head and his feet in the trash container for pickup and bury his feathers in the backyard," Julie said.

"In the first place Julie, nobody in my family likes cooked goose. Secondly, I don't think anybody in my family would be of a mind to cut off the goose's head," Devo said.

"We need somebody then to cut off the goose's head that could do it without any remorse. Let me think on that," Julie said as she rested her chin on the palm of her hand.

"What we need is somebody who can cut up an animal without really caring much about it; what about a butcher?" Julie said after much thought.

"That's a good idea Julie. Maybe we could get Mr. Hanna to take Jasontwo," Devo said smiling at Julie.

"I have it, Julie said, suppose you give the goose to Mr. Hanna free provided he gives you the feathers for a special project that you are working on. You could take the down and make a small pillow. I'm not sure what you would do with the big feathers," Julie said.

"With the big feathers I can make an Indian headpiece and a breastplate for my Boy Scout merit badge," Devo said anxiously.

"When I get down from my elephant, I can use the down from my goose to make a down pillow for Speeler to use in his dog house," Devo said laughing at Julie.

Chapter 27

SEPARATING THE PARTS

After school on Monday, Devo did not ride the school bus. It was only a short walk down to Mr. Hanna's butcher shop.

"Good afternoon Mr. Hanna, are you very busy right now?" Devo asked.

"No, as a matter of fact things are usually pretty slow on Monday."

"I see that you sell lamb, pork, chicken and fish; do you ever sell goose?" Devo asked.

"Very seldom Devo, once in a great while I get a request for goose for Thanksgiving or Christmas and that's about the only time, I buy one" Mr. Hanna replied.

"Thanksgiving will be here in a couple of weeks Mr. Hanna and I have a goose that I need to sell and I was wondering if you might be interested in buying it?" Devo asked.

"It might be nice to have a goose in my showcase for the Thanksgiving holiday. How much do you want for it Devo?"

"I would like to get three dollars for it Mr. Hanna."

"Oh! Devo that goose is worth much more than three dollars."

"The reason I am going to sell the goose so cheap is because there are a couple of conditions affecting the sale, Devo said.

"What are the conditions, Devo?"

"I would need to have all of the feathers from the goose," Devo said. "Might I ask what you want the feathers for Devo?"

"With the big feathers, after I color them, I plan to make an Indian headdress for Boy Scouts. With the down I plan to make a small soft pillow for my dog Speeler."

"Sounds like a worthy cause Devo. You bring in the goose and I will give you the three dollars. When the feathers are ready, I will call your house and let you know," Mr. Hanna said.

"Might I ask why your mother doesn't cook the goose, Devo?" Mr. Hanna asked.

"Nobody in my family felt that they could kill the goose and then eat it."

"I can understand that Devo, so you bring the goose in any time now and I will dress him and put him in my display case." Mr. Hanna said. "You are going to dress him?" Devo asked curiously.

"It's a butcher's term, Devo. It means to remove all the feathers and prepare the bird for cooking," Mr. Hanna said.

"By the way Devo, if I give you a bone will you take it home with you and give it to Speeler?"

"I would be glad to do that Mr. Hanna and thank you so much, I know Speeler will really appreciate it," Devo said.

When Devo arrived home after his walk from the butcher shop, he changed his clothes, had a snack and went out to the barn to find Speeler.

"Unwrap my bone so I can eat it," Speeler barked excitingly.

"How did you know I had a bone for you Speeler?" Devo asked.

"It's a dog thing, Devo, I could smell that bone the minute you entered the barn," Speeler Barked as he sniffed the air wagging his tail and waiting patiently for Devo to unwrap his bone from Mr. Hanna.

"Let's go up in the hayloft Speeler. I have something I need to talk to you about in privacy, where we won't be heard by Jasontwo," Devo said.

"Can I take my bone?"

"I will carry it up for you and unwrap it when we get to the top of the hayloft so it doesn't get dirty," Devo said.

When Devo and Speeler got to the very top of the hayloft they both laid down on their stomach. Devo unwrapped the dog bone from Mr. Hanna and gave it to Speeler.

Devo told Speeler about this trip to the butcher shop and his arrangements to sell Jasontwo to Mr. Hanna.

"I will need your help Speeler to get Jasontwo in the dog traveling cage and into the feed sack. Jasontwo may be getting wise to our little routine by now," Devo said.

"I think if I get close enough to the cage, he won't be able to resist the opportunity to bite my nose," Speeler barked as he chewed on his bone.

"Okay then, we will do this early Saturday morning and hopefully we will finally be rid of Jasontwo."

"Are you going to ask Julie to help us?" Speeler barked.

"I don't need a girl to help me, you and I can handle a simple job like this, Speeler," Devo said.

"I think you're forgetting this whole thing was Julie's idea. She helped us out when neither one of us could think of a way to get rid of Jasontwo." Speeler barked. "I don't see it that way, Speeler."

"I think you are afraid to admit that she is a very smart girl and you like her." Speeler barked.

"Yeah, yeah, yeah but I don't happen to share your opinion," Devo said in a simpering voice.

Chapter 28

SEEKING ADVICE

Saturday morning Devo was up early, ate breakfast and ran out to the barn to wake Speeler up. Devo loaded the dog traveling cage into his wagon along with an empty feed sack.

Devo opened the cage door and crept up to the dog house from behind and quickly placed the cage with the open door over the entrance to the dog house.

Speeler ran up to the cage and started barking. Jasontwo was up on his feet, out the front door of the dog house, flapping his wings, honking and squawking as loud as he could. As he entered the dog travel cage his outstretched wing caught on the cage and pulled it away from the dog house. Jasontwo took advantage of the situation and he scurried out into the yard.

Speeler had not expected Jasontwo to get out of the dog traveling cage and stood there in amazement without moving as Jasontwo came up and bit him on the nose. When Devo saw what was happening, he ran over to Speeler to protect his dog from this vicious goose.

Jasontwo took the opportunity to bite Devo's hand once again.

Jasontwo then flew up to the top of the dog house where he continued to honk and squawk in a loud voice.

"Is my nose bleeding?" Speeler barked as he brushed his nose with his paws.

"Yes, I'm afraid so. I do see just a little bit of blood," Devo said.

"Is your finger bleeding?" Speeler barked.

"It's not bleeding but it is swollen and pretty sore," Devo said as he held his finger up for Speeler to inspect.

"Now what Mr. Magician?" Speeler Barked anxiously.

"I don't think we are going to be able to capture Jasontwo while he is sitting on top of the dog house so we will need to come up with another plan." Devo said.

"I hate to bring this up again but why don't we walk down to Julie's house and see what she has to say about catching Jasontwo, Speeler barked." Devo stood silently as he looked at the goose sitting on top Speeler's dog house.

Devo sat down in the grass about 20 feet away from the dog house.

Devo just sat there without saying anything and finally after about 5 minutes Speeler came and sat down alongside him.

"This is not going to be as easy as I thought it would be," Devo mumbled begrudgingly to his dog.

As the two would-be goose capturers sat and looked on at Jasontwo sitting on top of the dog house, Speeler barked, "This may call for some high-powered magical spell."

"Magic is what got me into this predicament, Devo said, I think we need to resort to a different method to handle this situation, "Devo said.

"Julie?" Speeler Barked as he looked up at Devo.

"I believe you are right," Devo said.

When Devo arrived at the Meyers home, he knocked at the front door and asked for Julie.

"I believe Julie's in the back yard playing in the tree house," Mrs. Meyers said.

Speeler and Devo walked to the back yard of the Meyer home and when they got to the tree house Devo called Julie.

When They Got To The Tree House Devo Called Julie

"Hi Devo, do you and Speeler Want To come up and play dolls with me?"

"Not really," Devo muttered.

"Well, what do you want then?" Julie asked.

Speeler has a problem and he would like you to help him" Devo said.

"Speeler has a problem, huh? Are you sure you don't have a problem?" Julie asked.

"If you can come down from the tree house, I will tell you what the problem is," Devo said.

Julie climbed down from the treehouse and sat on the ground and motioned for Devo and Speeler to come and sit beside her.

"Well, what is the problem that Speeler is having?" Julie asked.

"It seems that Jason to has taken over Speeler's dog house and will not let him in."

"Speeler told you this?" Julie asked.

"Well...." "You have a talking dog now, huh?"

"Well....," Devo mumbled.

"Well, why don't you tell me what your problem is Speeler, Julie said smiling.

Speeler barked.

"Oh! I am so sorry Speeler; I didn't understand what you said. Your dog does talk doesn't he, Devo?" Julie said sarcastically.

"Well....," Devo mumbled again.

"Why don't you just tell me what it is you want Devo Mannix," Julie said very blunt and direct.

"Well...."

"Well what?" Julie said.

"Well, okay, I will tell you. We were trying to catch Jasontwo this morning and get him in the dog traveling cage and he got away. He is now setting on top of Speeler's dog house and he is not likely to come down. We need to catch him so we can take him to Mr. Hanna."

"Speeler and I have run out of ideas and we were wondering if you can help us?"

Julie sat for a long time without saying anything. Finally, she said,

"You and Speeler go home, keep your eye on Jasontwo and I will be there in a little bit," Julie said.

"What are you going to do, Julie?" Devo asked.

"We are going fishing!" Julie said.

"That's how we got in so much trouble in the beginning, Julie. Are we going to get in more trouble fishing with you?" Devo asked hesitantly.

"You and Speeler go home, keep your eye on Jasontwo. Go in front of the dog house and keep his attention on you. I will be there in a little bit," Julie said.

"Are you sure?" Devo asked.

"Positive," Julie said bluntly.

Chapter 29

FISHING AGAIN

Devo and Speeler went back to the house. Devo picked up a stick that had fallen from one of the trees.

Speeler stood in front of the dog house and barked. Devo waved the sticks and called to Jasontwo to get his attention. Jasontwo honked, hissed and honked but he did not move from his perch on top of the dog house.

Devo and Speeler had been in front of the dog house getting Jasontwo's attention for over 10 minutes when Julie appeared, coming from the woods from behind the dog house.

Julie was bent over and slowly moved to the rear of the dog house. "I have you now," Julie said as she threw her father's landing net over Jasontwo whose attention had been centered on Devo and Speeler.

Julie Threw Her Father's Landing Net Over Jasontwo.

"Bring the feed sack Devo and help me put Jasontwo in the bag," Julie said excitedly.

Devo ran to the dog house carrying the feed sack.

"Reach under the landing net and grab Jasontwo by his feet," Julie said breathlessly.

"Devo reached under the landing net, grabbed Jasontwo by the feet and put him in the feed sack.

"I have you now" Devo said breathlessly.

"Great job, Julie and Devo," Speeler barked.

"That was great thinking Julie, where did you get the landing net?" Devo asked.

"It belongs to my dad. He uses it when he goes salmon fishing in Canada every year," Julie responded.

"I am going to put Jasontwo in the dog carrying cage just in case he might get out of the feed sack," Devo said.

Devo, with the help of Julie, put Jasontwo into the dog carrying cage and set it in the wagon.

"We need to go to the butcher shop now Julie. Would you like to go with us?" Devo said politely.

"I would love to do that Devo, but I must return my father's landing net on the way to the butcher shop."

Julie, Devo and Speeler walked down the street and after a stop at Julie's house to return the landing net, they pulled the wagon containing Jasontwo to the front door of Mr. Hanna's butcher shop.

"Good morning Mr. Hanna; I have my goose outside in the wagon, shall I bring him in?" Devo asked.

"That will be fine Devo, bring him in and I will put him in the back room until I am ready," Mr. Hanna said.

Devo brought the goose in and laid it on the meat block for Mr. Hanna.

Mr. Hanna went over to the cash register and withdrew three dollars.

"Here is your three dollars Devo; as agreed."

"It has been a pleasure to do business with you," Mr. Hanna said as he handed Devo the three dollars.

"I have a doggie bone for Speeler; will you give it to him Devo?" Mr. Hanna asked.

"He is right outside, I'm sure he will be thrilled to death; thank you very much."

Devo gave the dog bone to Speeler and the three of them started to walk back to Devo's house.

Suddenly, Speeler put his bone down on the sidewalk, perked up his ears and barked, "I hear the ice cream man coming."

"What is Speeler barking about?" Julie asked.

"He hears the ice cream man coming,"

"I don't hear anything," Julie said.

"Believe me; if Speeler says the ice cream man is coming you can count on it." Devo said.

It wasn't long before both Julie and Devo heard the ice cream wagon come around the corner playing, "Pop! Goes the weasel."

As soon as the ice cream wagon approached; Speeler walked out into the center of the road, sat down wagged his tail and barked.

The ice cream man stopped opened his side panel and asked, "What will you have?"

"I would like three Eskimo Pies," Devo said.

The ice cream man turned, opened the lid of the freezer and pulled out three Eskimo Pies.

"That will be $4.50."

Devo took two dollars from his wallet and the three dollars he got from Mr. Hanna and paid for the Eskimo Pies.

"Keep the change," Devo said smiling at the ice cream man. It has been a really great day."

The ice cream man thanked Devo, shut the side panel door and drove off.

Devo handed one of the Eskimo Pies to Julie and said, "Thank you Julie, for all your help. We would have never caught Jasontwo if you had not brought the fish landing net to catch him," Devo said.

"Speeler, if you put your doggie bone down, I will unwrap this Eskimo Pies and give it to you."

Devo unwrapped the Eskimo Pie and held it so Speeler could eat it. When Speeler was finished, Devo unwrapped his own Eskimo Pie and the three of them continued their journey to Devo's home.

Chapter 30

AN UNBELIEVABLE MYSTERY

About three weeks had passed since Devo sold his goose to Mr. Hanna. With the help of Thunder Cloud, a Native American Cree Indian, a client of Devo's father; Devo was able to make his Indian headdress and breast plate.

Using the hollow end of the big wing feathers along with some beads and colored string from an arts and crafts store, Devo was able to fashion his small breasts plate.

The remainder of the larger wing and tail feathers were used to make a Cree powwow head dress.

Devo's mother using an old sheet made a pillow case for Devo. Devo stuffed the pillowcase with the down from the goose's breast feathers to fashion a pillow for Speeler's dog house.

"Well how do you like your down pillow?" Devo asked.

"I love it; it is so soft and warm at night. The thing I like the most about it is when I think that we finally got rid of Jasontwo," Speeler barked.

The bark was hardly out of Speeler's mouth when out of the woods came a white goose.

The goose walked up to Speeler's dog house, ate the remainder of the food in his doggie dish, took a drink of water, flapped his wings and perched himself on top of Speeler's dog house.

"Looks like I'll be sleeping in the barn again tonight," Speeler barked. "I can't believe it. Will I never be able to get rid of the goose that I created?" Devo said sadly.

"I think you need to talk to your grandfather," Speeler barked. "I'm wondering now if something that we use for one of our incantations already had a spell on it," Devo said.

When Devo and Speeler arrived at the front of the house Grandfather was sitting in the porch swing drinking his morning coffee.

"I have a problem Grandfather and I need your help," Devo said. "What's the problem, Devo?" Grandfather said.

Devo told his grandfather the events from the beginning starting with the orca, ending up with the incantation to create Jasontwo and his recent return.

"I'm wondering now if something that we use for one of our incantations already had a spell on it," Devo said.

"That's always a possibility and I know of no way to determine in advance if a spell really already exists," Grandfather said.

"Do you have any suggestions, Grandfather?"

"Let's not rush into anything at the moment Devo. Let's be kind to the goose, feed him, see that he has water and perhaps we will come up with an answer to the problem that will solve it for once and forever.

"Thank you, Grandfather, I will take your advice." Devo said.

Every morning before the goose was awake and out of the dog house Devo would creep silently up to Speeler's food dish and fill it. After refilling the water dish with fresh water Devo would return silently to the house without waking the goose.

The next morning at breakfast Grandfather told Devo that he should go down to the butcher shop and talk to Mr. Hanna to see if he had really sold Jasontwo and gave you his feathers or if perhaps he kept Jasontwo and gave you the feathers from some other goose.

As Jason and Speeler walked down Shady Lane headed for the butcher shop they met Julie walking up the road towards their house. "Where are you going today, Devo?" Julie asked.

"Hi Julie; we are headed to Mr. Hanna's Butcher Shop to find out if the feathers he gave me were really from Jasontwo," Devo said.

"Why would you think they are not the feathers from Jasontwo?" Julie asked.

"Because Julie, there is a white goose sitting on top of Speeler's dog house as we speak."

"How do you know it's Jasontwo?" Julie asked.

"Because it's a white goose sitting on top of Speeler's dog house. "What you're telling me Devo, is that all horses are animals therefore, all animals are horses," Julie said smiling.

"That's dumb Julie, is this one of those elephant things? I just know its Jasontwo," Devo said.

"I'll bet you it isn't Jasontwo," Julie said with a very positive tone of voice.

"Well, I'll bet you it is Jasontwo, Devo said in an irritated voice.

"Okay, I'll bet you it isn't Jasontwo and if it is not, you will... Julie hesitated to think and then she said, "You will play dolls with me all day next Saturday."

"Deal and if you lose you will...You will clean up Speeler's little messes in my entire yard on Saturday.

"Deal! Be at my house no later than 8:30 a.m., so we will have time to play with all my dolls," Julie said, smiling.

"Yes! And you bring a shovel and a plastic bag and be at my house no later than 8:30 a.m. Saturday morning.

"So where are you going, Devo?"

"We're going in the butcher shop to see Mr. Hanna."

Chapter 31

THE MYSTERY IS SOLVED

Good morning Julie and Devo. To what do I owe the pleasure of your visit to my butcher shop?" Mr. Hanna said as he welcomed the children. "Good morning, Mr. Hanna," Devo said.

"What can I do for you this morning?"

"I came to ask you about the goose I sold you," Devo said.

"What would you like to know Devo," Mr. Hanna asked.

"I need to know about the feathers Mr. Hanna. Were all of them from the goose I sold you?" Devo asked.

"Every last one of them came from your goose, Devo. I removed all the feathers in my shed, put them in a plastic bag and tied the top," Mr. Hanna said.

"Is there a problem Devo?" Mr. Hanna asked.

"I was just wondering if it might be possible that some other feathers might have gotten mixed in with the ones you gave me," Devo said.

"Hardly possible Devo, I never dress any feathered birds in my shop; I always do them at home in my shed."

"Why do you ask, Devo?"

"No particular reason Mr. Hanna I was just curious. Thank you again Mr. Hanna, I have to go now," Devo said as he turned to leave the butcher shop.

When Devo and Julie returned to Devo's home, they were surprised to find a strange car parked in the driveway and a man and three small children standing on the porch talking to Grandfather.

When Julie and Devo walked up to the front porch Grandfather said, "Devo this is Mr. Plumber and he would like to talk to you about your goose."

Devo walked up to Mr. Plumber shook his hand, introduced Julie and his dog Speeler.

"What can I tell you about my goose Mr. Plumber?" Devo asked.

"After talking to your grandfather Devo, I believe that the goose you have is mine. I believe he is the goose that my children have raised from an egg they hatched in science class at school," Mr. Plumber said.

"That would be wonderful news if the goose sitting on Speeler's dog house is truly yours, but how will we be able to tell?" Devo asked.

"If you don't mind Devo, I would like to take my children back and let them call Mr. Honk to see if she will come to them," Mr. Plumber said.

Looking at the three children Devo said, "If you will follow me, I'll take you back to where the goose is setting," Devo said.

Everybody walked into the backyard and when the children were about 10 feet from Speeler's dog house one of them said, "Here Honk, here Mr. Honker.

The goose immediately jumped off of Speeler's dog house and walked to the little boy calling him. When he was about 1 foot away from the little boy, the boy picked him up and held him in his arms.

Devo could tell immediately that the goose belonged to the Plumber children.

"I believe he is yours," Grandfather Mannix said to Mr. Plumber.

The children loaded Mr. Honker into the backseat of the car and after thanking Devo and Grandfather they headed down the driveway.

"I was beginning to believe in the supernatural Grandfather, I was wondering how that goose could keep coming back and sit on Speeler's dog house," Devo said.

"Animals like geese, like to perch off the ground so they can see you and what's going on. Since Speeler's dog house is probably the highest thing in the backyard it is just natural that they would use that to perch on," Grandfather said.

"Devo looked at Julie and said, "You were right all along Julie. That really wasn't my goose.

"I need to go home now Julie said. Be at my house promptly at 8:30 a.m., Saturday."

"Speeler, I hate playing dolls with girls," Devo said.

"Well! I think the important thing to remember here is "Have you learned anything from this fishing adventure?" Speeler barked.

"Yes, I think I have," Devo said.

"And what would that be, Devo?"

"One: don't make bets with girls; Two: when your dog tells you that he knows all there is to know about fishing because he watched one episode of Fishing with Fred Wilson, go seek help from another source.

Three: follow the instructions."

"Did you learn anything, Speeler?"

"I learned one thing," Speeler barked.

"And what is that?" Devo asked.

"It is better not to bark and let everyone think you are a dumb dog, than to bark and remove any doubt."

About the Author

Roland Vincent Boike was born October 28, 1930 at his family home in Madeira, Ohio.

During the Korean War, Roland served in the 147th Field Artillery Battalion.

Roland attended Western Kentucky State University, Ohio State Department of Agriculture, and the University of Cincinnati Department of Applied Arts.

He was awarded a full scholarship to attend Lincoln College of Chiropractic where he graduated in 1962 with a Degree in Chiropractic.

Roland practiced Chiropractic in Loveland, Ohio for thirty- five years and was a Staff Physician at Jewish Hospital in Kenwood, Ohio. He served as Team Physician for Loveland High School, Western Brown High School and Wilmington College Girls Soccer Team.

Roland served as Mayor and Vice Mayor in Loveland, Ohio.

Roland was a founder and a Director of The Community National Bank in Loveland, Ohio. He was Chairman of the Loveland 1976 Centennial Celebration, which produced a live outdoor spectacular, "The History of Loveland".

Roland was a founder, past president and member of the Board of Trustees of The Loveland Chamber of Commerce. Roland is the originator of the Loveland Valentine program and coined the phrase "There Is Nothing in This World So Sweet as Love".

He was recognized with an award from The National Safety Council for saving the lives of three children in a submerged automobile at Lake Isabella in May, 1964.

Roland was honored by the City of Loveland, Ohio for dedicated service to the community with a commemorative marker In the Veteran's Memorial Park and the Loveland Biking and Hiking Trail.

Roland is a Kentucky Colonel and has received numerous awards for civic achievements.